FRIEND REQUEST

A NOVEL BY

K.T. Thompson

Social media has taken over people's lives. Many people use it in many different ways. Here are 4 different characters who use it as they see fit. I'm pretty sure the characters in "Friend Request" will remind you of someone on your friends list. Each of these characters uses social media in their own unique way. Follow (Kei Kei 16), (Mario 33), (Shanell 39), and (Jasonic 27) as they take you on twists and turns in the social media world of "Friend Request."

Kei Kei

7:47 AM Kei Kei was sitting in the principal's office at her high school, Maynard Evans High School, in a rough section of Orlando known as Pine Hills.

The first period bell rang at 7:40 letting the kids know that they should start heading to their first class of the day, but while it was ringing Kei Kei was already on top of Kayla (AKA LaLa) beating her like she had stolen something. This was Kei Kei's 3rd fight this year—her junior year.

School was only in its second trimester, and she had already been suspended twice before for fights and arguments. The Principal had warned her, her mother Tanya, and her Probation Officer Mrs. Washington, that if she were to get into another fight she would be facing possible expulsion.

Kei Kei had a legendary reputation as a fighter. She was a social media sensation as several of her fights had been downloaded so that the world could see her in action. Her temper always seemed to be on edge as she was known to go from 0-60 in the blink of an eye. Her attitude was just as toxic and many people steered clear of her, because she was known for spazzing out on most. She had 5000 friends on Facebook, and over 20,000 people following her posts, a lot of them in other cities and states. She also had an assortment of Twerk videos, sneak diss videos, shade videos, and videos dropping names, secrets, and rumors. She had a huge following on Instagram, Twitter and Snapchat as well.

Just two years earlier she was known as the little girl who was walking around Meadowbrook Middle school pregnant and who had birthed a child while there. As she sat there in Principal Barnett's office she had a lot to think about and some explaining to do. She was allowed to make a phone call so she called her Mama and her Probation Officer.

LaLa, the girl that she had just punished with a brutal beating, was down at the school nurse's station getting her wounds attended to. Her Mom had also been called. Kei Kei had beaten her unmercifully. It took the school resource officer and two Evans High football players to pull Kei Kei off of that girl. Kei Kei felt like she had brought it on herself, because it wasn't like she hadn't warned her, like she had warned so many others before she gave them the business. LaLa was one of Kei Kei's 5000 Facebook friends. She also followed her on Facebook as well so she could see all of her posts. So in Kei Kei's eyes she had no excuse as to why she had jumped on her early this morning before first period class.

Most people who knew and followed Kei Kei knew about Prince her two-year-old son, whom she always posted pictures of but rarely kept. And they knew about Super Dave, her Haitian boyfriend and baby daddy. Kei Kei had already stepped to LaLa before and asked her nicely to stop "liking" everything that Super Dave posted. Kei Kei was fed up with this little hoe. If Super Dave posted a random picture she would like it with a heart emoji. If he posted a club picture she would like it with an eggplant emoji. LaLa would hit like on any and everything that her man/baby daddy would post.

So after Kei Kei had snapped on Super Dave about this little hoe, and stepped to LaLa and confronted her about all of her likes and emoji's, she felt that she had given both of them warning shots. The next time she would come out firing on the both of them.

Then it happened. Super Dave and she were having sex when she heard the inbox on his desktop computer ding from someone leaving a message on his open Facebook page. Kei Kei acted as if she didn't hear and continued to have sex. She knew that he had heard it though, because he briefly stopped hitting her from the back for a quick second or two. As soon as they were done having sex and Super Dave went to the bathroom to shower and wash up, she went over to the desktop computer and looked at the screen. She saw where LaLa had violated again. She read the message that LaLa had left inside his inbox. "What's up, stranger? I see you don't fw me no more Kei Kei must be sexing you good. Pull up on me and come fw a real bitch like me and smoke some of that good shit you be having, and afterwards it's whatever. LOL, smiley face emoji, wink face emoji, eggplant emoji."

Kei Kei was 38 hot, she knew right then and there she was going to run up on this little hoe LaLa and teach her some manners the next day when they got back to school. She said to herself, "This bitch is gonna give me one on sight."

Just then, she heard Super Dave coming out of the bathroom from showering. As he walked out at first she was mad and wanted to go in on his ass about him messaging back and forth with this lil hoe LaLa, but she didn't want to start an argument with him. After all LaLa was sweating him, just like all the rest of the hoes she had jumped on, beat up, and ran off over the past 2 years.

She loved her man/baby daddy. He was a 21-year-old drug dealer and fraud scam artist who had clout and street cred. He walked out in only a towel wrapped around his black sexy Haitian self, and Kei Kei forgot that she was mad at him too. She wanted to go for a round two, but while he was in the shower, her Mom Tanya had called and was cussing and fussing about her getting her ass home to spend some quality time with her two year old son. Tanya had also reminded her about her 8 o'clock probation curfew.

So instead of asking Super Dave for a round two of sex she asked him to roll and smoke a blunt with her on his way taking her home. When they pulled up in front of the apartments Kei Kei and Tanya lived in, Super Dave was going to get out and come in and see his son Prince for a few minutes, but his phone rang. It was his partner and right-hand man Teddy calling him, letting him know that they had a lick to go and surveillance. At first Kei Kei was mad, but she knew any time Teddy called that Super Dave was going to go and see what his partner was talking about, but she also knew that whenever Teddy called, Super Dave always came up on a come up. He kissed her and gave her some money to buy their son Prince some new Jordans and told her he would call her later.

The next day while students were still getting off the buses, right before the first period bell could be heard, Kei Kei spotted LaLa coming up the main hallway. She quickly made a beeline for her, ran up on her, and hit her like a linebacker blitz. Poor LaLa, she never saw the blitz coming and she went down like a quarterback with poor peripheral vision. LaLa couldn't do anything with Kei Kei's little cocky strong self all over her. This wouldn't have been a fair fight head on, but it was clearly a molly wop after Kei Kei ran up on her unexpectedly and Lawrence Taylor'd her.

While she was sitting in the Principals office Kei Kei kept seeing many of her friends and classmates come through the main office where the Principal's office was, look through the plate glass window, and laugh in favor of what she had just done to LaLa. She heard them out there saying that they had video taped the whole thing, and that they were going to download it on Facebook and Instagram. Just that fast, Kei Kei smiled and wondered how many likes she would get on Facebook. She thought about all of the comments people would make about how she had dish-ragged LaLa.

At that precise moment, she saw her Mom Tanya come walking through the door of the main office holding a sleeping Prince in her arms, and she did not look happy. Tanya at 32 years old was still young enough to be Prince's mom, but instead she was the grandmom. She had become pregnant with Kei Kei at 16 years old, when she was a student at Evans herself. How ironic it was for her to be back here at the same high school she used to attend, trying to check on the same child that she was pregnant with when she was a student there. Tanya was pointed to the Principals office where her daughter was sitting, she walked through the door and looked over at her daughter Kei Kei who had her head down. She went over to her, and was about to try and find out what had happened, when the door she had walked in just moments ago swung open and in walked another parent, a young girl with knots, scrapes, and bruises all over her head and face, and the school resource officer.

Mario

Mario had Tina's legs high in the air giving her the pokes she had poked him on Facebook and said she wanted several times. They were at his favorite hotel, the Geneva, where you paid for your room by the hour. He would only need an hour or two at the most. He figured he would just give this lil thirsty THOT what they both wanted, some sex. Mario felt as if he was just donating to the many young, naive, impressionable females whom he had fooled on Facebook, Instagram and Snapchat.

Mario was a smooth, well-dressed, well-groomed brother who put pressure on thirsty attention-seeking chicks by posting pictures with large stacks of money, nice cars with rims on them, and travel to nice places like Jamaica or Miami. He posted pictures in all of the latest brand clothing.

He masqueraded on social media as an entrepreneurial business man, community activist, and father figure. But all of these characters were just personas that he made up to fool people of the lies he was living. Mario was a cocaine, weed, and pill supplier who hid behind these characters to keep the feds and local law enforcement off of him He was the father of two kids. One was an 11-year-old son whose mother had been killed in a home invasion 9 years earlier where the robbers were targeting. He also had an 8-year-old daughter with his current fiancée, Tegina.

Mario had taken Orlando by storm, his name was ringing in the high levels of the streets in Orlando, and also the low-level drug world as well. Not many people knew him when he burst back upon the scene out of nowhere. He had quietly gone away into obscurity after those thugs ran off into his house and killed his lady. But now people were talking about him again, because of his newfound social media fame. He started getting instant attention and Facebook and Instagram fame as soon as he started posting a flashy, boastful lifestyle.

That's why Tina was here now getting dug out in an hourly hotel, even though she herself had a fiance at home. Tina was one of those supposed bad bitches that got catfished all the time by looking at the grass in other yards, instead of tending to and treating the grass in her own yard. Tina was just like millions of other women that thought they knew people just by viewing their profile and the things that they posted. Two people who barely knew each other were in a sleazy hotel having sex like they had known each other for years, both cheating on their fiances and doing the same things sexually that they were doing to their fiances. Tina knew that Mario had a fiancee, because he had plenty of pictures of Tegina, claiming her as his fiancee in his photos. Mario knew that she had a fiance as well.

Tina ran with a group of women that all snuck behind their men's back and were side chicks to other ballers, players, and drug dealers. She was just another notch in Mario's belt. He knew that she would run back to her whorish clique bragging about having slept with him. He knew that her clique was full of hoes that would backdoor each other so her running back and telling them was fine with him, he would just start picking them all off one by one, or better yet get some threesomes going with these hoes. As he flipped her and put her in position after position he knew that he had another one wrapped around his finger. He told her to get down on her knees and give him some sloppy head and just like a star-struck groupie she did as she was told. She was all into it too, sloppily sucking this man as if this wasn't their first time being together on a sexual encounter.

Little did Tina know she was starring in a reality TV show that wasn't a part of her reality. Mario was secretly videotaping and recording her just like he did all of the sexual conquests he had fooled from off social media. He was going to put them all on World Star Hip Hop, Vlad TV, or even Porn Hub if any of them ever got out of hand or famous, or if he ever went broke. He targeted mostly the women that were already in relationships, because he knew that they couldn't raise hell about him when they were already in relationships themselves. He would laugh at the screen every Monday when some of these same chicks that were doing the exact same things as Tina was here doing now, would make their husbands, fiances, boyfriends, and baby daddies their MCM (man crush monday). He orgasmed in her mouth and she just kept right on sucking. He fell back on the bed and damn near had to beat her off of his manhood. A big sinister smile crept across her face as she thought to herself "Job well done."

Mario saw the satisfied smile on her face and thought to himself, "I bet that this nasty hoe is going to go right home and kiss her MCM right in the mouth." All while the camera he had set up and running kept recording.

Shanell

Shanell hugged her 18-year-old daughter Madison (AKA Maddy) in a tight embrace. For the first time in their lives they were about to be separated for an extended period of time. She was going to really, really, really, miss her daughter and only child Maddy, but man was she ready to get back home to Orlando. She had spent the entire weekend up in Tallahassee getting Maddy set up and settled in at Florida A & M University, also known as FAMU. Shanell was more like an older sister to Maddy than a mother. She had accumulated more friends Maddy's age than she had friends her own age.

Maddy's father Domonique was in the fifteenth year of a 33-year Federal prison sentence he had received for being the ring leader of a cocaine smuggling ring. Not only was Domonique Maddy's father, he was also the love of Shanell's life and the only man she had ever made love to up to that point in her life. He was her first and only boyfriend, and even up until the age of 16 she wasn't able to date, talk to boys, or give out her home phone number. All throughout high school she had to sneak to be in a relationship with Domonique. They carried on a 3-year high school relationship under both of their parents' noses, by communicating and only being together at school. They both attended West Orange high school in Winter Garden, Florida, just 5 minutes west of Orlando.

Shanell and Domonique spent every minute that they could together walking around the campus together at West Orange. From the moment her bus dropped her off at the school and his dropped him off at the school they would mingle around and wait for the other to arrive. Then Domonique would walk Shanell to her first period class and head towards his before the bell rang. This would continue all throughout the school day, and then at the end of the school day they would walk down to the bus terminal and wait for their prospective buses together. They kissed passionately before they went their separate ways, all to do it all again the next day. They both hated weekends, holidays, and the end of the school year, because they took some of their precious together time away from them.

Domonique was a light-skinned, cat-eyed Virgin Islands native who was not born in America. He arrived on U.S soil at the age of 13, and quickly adapted his father's working mentality. Shanell was a dark-skinned, slim-thick Jamaican chick, with long dreadlocks down her back, who rarely talked or spoke to anyone. Shanell was born and raised here in the States, but her dad was a real-deal Jamaican Rastafarian who still in spite of not being in his homeland raised his kids as if they were. We call them Jamericans.

In the separate parts of Winter Garden where Shanell had grown up, and where Domonique was brought up and living, Virgin Islanders and Jamaicans didn't like each other, and had very little to do with the other. Domonique's father was a data entry specialist at a large military program in Orlando. He was teaching his son Domonique how to trade stock options, work numbers on NASDAQ, and making investments. Growing up he knew of his father's hatred and disdain for Jamaicans. He had heard him say on many occasions that they were lazy, barbaric, violent drug runners who only wanted to smoke and grow marijuana. Shanell's father was a long-distance truck driver who owned his own rig. He leased and contracted his services out to a long list of long haul companies. He and his Jamaican cohorts didn't care too much for Virgin Islanders either. They looked at them as goody-two-shoes who were afraid to get their hands dirty, or bloody for that matter. Shanell's father was a truck driver second, because what he was first was a trafficker. The only reason why he owned and drove his big rig was to move large shipments of illegal drugs and narcotics for the many drug lords who acquired his services. He drove all over the United States all throughout the years, and at 56 years old he planned to drive until 70 and then retire with a nice fat nest egg. Shanell was ready to get back home in Ocoee, and sleep in her own bed.

Sonic

Sonic was on his phone surfing his Facebook and Instagram accounts, checking the traps that he had baited and set a couple months earlier. Jasonic "Sonic" Hayes was a vicious robber/jack boy who robbed drug dealers and ballers for a living. He was looking at a picture he had set up on a fake page he had made to allow him to stalk his victims. The name on the profile picture was "Club Promoter Jay." He had also set up a fake account on Instagram too. The actual guy in the pictures was one of his money-getting friends he had grown up with in Detroit with who was doing Federal prison time up north. Sonic knew that no one down south in Florida knew his homie Slow Money as he was called, so he made the fake profile up under Club Promoter Jay. He knew that people put their guards down when it came to club promoters, because they were known and affiliated with bringing fun, not causing chaos.

Sonic had fled Detroit after he was acquitted on a triple murder case. He hadn't beat the case because he was innocent; he beat it on a technicality. The moment he and his co-defendant were found not guilty and were released from jail they were both marked for death by the family members of the three high-profile drug dealers they had tortured and killed. They both had ten-thousand-dollar bounties on their heads. His co-defendant Pee Wee never even made it halfway home. The taxicab that had arrived at the jail to pick him and Sonic up after they were to be released was carjacked and found burning with his body still inside an hour later. Dental records later confirmed that it was in fact Paul James (AKA Pee Wee). The only thing that saved Sonic's life that night was a clerical mistake down at the courthouse. Pee Wee was released a few hours earlier than him and it cost him his life.

After the Detroit Bureau of Investigations came in and ruled Pee Wee's death as a kidnapping and execution style murder, they knew that they had to try and protect a vicious murderer whom they had arrested themselves for doing the exact same thing to others. They took him downtown to one of their safehouses and convinced him to find another state to start his life over in because if he stayed in Detroit he was definitely a dead man. They had gotten wind of the ten-thousand-dollar bounty on his head. That had told him that he didn't have to allow someone to collect it as they had already done on his co-defendant Pee Wee. They knew that every thug, hood, con man, and even some drug dealers, including some of Sonic's own family and friends, were going to try and collect on it. Sonic told them that he had a father that stayed in Orlando, Florida. Before he could tell them that he hadn't seen his father in years and that he didn't even know what part of Orlando he stayed in, or even know if he was still living there or alive at all, the Mayor of Detroit was signing off on putting Sonic on a private plane flight, with 5000 dollars in undocumented, unregistered cash. They were paying a small price to make a big problem go away.

When Sonic's plane landed at Orlando International Airport, he didn't know whether to go to the right or the left. Sonic instantly noticed that there were a whole bunch of similarities between his hometown Detroit and Orlando. They were similar in size, similar in mixed cultures, and crime ridden. He liked Orlando already. Just like Detroit, Orlando had four sides. A black side, a white side, a black/Hispanic side, and a white/Hispanic side. While standing there pondering which way to go, he spotted a black airport porter and told him to point him to the predominantlyy black section of Orlando. Thirty minutes later Sonic was in a cab that pulled up to Texas Avenue and Americana Blvd. This looked like the perfect place for Sonic to blend in at. A wicked smile crept across his face as he gave the taxi cab driver his money and stepped into his new element. Pretty soon he would be back to his old ways.

Kei Kei

The bell had just rung and if Kei Kei didn't hurry up and hang up her phone call with Super Dave and get to class she was going to be late, again. She was attending her new school called CEP, her last chance at getting a high school diploma. Community Education Partners, or CEP as it was more commonly called, was a final chance for high-risk, at-risk, violent, falling-behind students. CEP was known for helping students that had been expelled from their public school system for fighting, weapons or drugs, gang membership and affiliation, and pregnancies. Kei Kei was now a student at CEP because this was her very last chance before the Orange County school board expelled her for good. The only reason why the school board felt compelled to give her this last chance was that her Guidance counselor at Evans, Mrs. Joyce Thompson, had been her Mom Tanya's guidance counselor 16 years earlier when Tanya was pregnant with Kei Kei. Mrs. Thompson pulled some strings for Kei Kei that gave her this last Hail Mary of a chance to get a high school diploma. Mrs. Thompson told the directors of the Orange County Board of Education that if Kei Kei was expelled it would be a violation of her probation, and the violation would send her away to a state program until she turned 19. She told them that Kei Kei was only a 16-year-old teen mom who didn't need to be away from her daughter for that long period of time. The Board felt sympathetic towards the baby Prince, not Kei Kei. But they elected to give her this one last chance, for the baby's sake. Kei Kei hung up the phone from talking to Super Dave and walked into her first period class and sat down at her desk just as the tardy bell rang. She was actually a very smart student who carried a 3.3 GPA. When she wasn't fighting, arguing, or embroiled in some turmoil about Super Dave and all of the social media mess. She was busy raising her hand and answering most of the trivia the teachers would bring up. Her first period class was an advanced algebra class, and it was one of her favorites. She put her phone on silent and placed it in her purse. It was learning time and once she was locked in on her studies, it would take a major crisis or disturbance to divert her attention from it.

Mario

A stretch limousine pulled up to Mario's house in a gated community. From out of his nice home walked Mario, being filmed on a live "Go Live" Facebook post. He was smiling because he loves the attention he draws from being in front of a camera. He threw up the deuces sign that Drake threw up in his "Deuces" video, all while walking to the stretch limo that was parked waiting in front of his house. He jumped inside the limo, rolled down the window nearest where he was seated in the back,,and said "Real niggas do real things," as the limo pulled away from the curb and disappeared.

Mario just knew that when people viewed his "Go Live" video on his Facebook and Instagram pages, his legend would grow even larger. In Mario's mind he was a Reality T.V. show star, without a major deal. So he decided to film everything himself and sooner or later someone would see one of his "Go Live" videos and recognize him as the star that he truly was. The only problem with Mario's way of thinking was, the camera wasn't always rolling on his unreal reality world. It was just rolling when he wanted it to be rolling. He didn't film his drug transactions.

Inside the limo Mario was in full actor mode on his "Go Live" Facebook feed. He was only going to Downtown Orlando and one of Club Promoter Tony Glover's soiree parties. He told any and everyone that was tuned in to his "Go Live" feed that he was riding solo dolo to the event because that's how he rolled. The camera was rolling as the limo pulled up to the club and he exited it just like the star celebrities going to the award shows in Hollywood and New York did. He was raising the bar to new heights on the flossing scene in Orlando. Mario didn't need a limo to take him to the club and drop him off—he had two luxury cars, a convertible dunk, and a luxury SUV at home parked in his 6-car garage. He just wanted to switch the game up on the girls and women that were impressed by material things. He was putting pressure on them to resist his temptings and stay focused on the relationships that they were already in. He knew that this stunt would get him more "Likes," "Pokes," and "Follows." He lived for this, it was an adrenaline rush, like an orgasm of epic proportions. Attention and money was of extreme importance to him.

He got out of the limo near the long line that was waiting near the entrance to get inside the club. He walked past that line and was escorted to a side VIP entrance as the males mean mugged him, and the females gawked at him in awe. Tony Glover had told Mario an hour earlier on the phone to have his limo bring him around to the side entrance so he wouldn't have to fight the large crowd to get in and make it to the VIP section. All the while he was being led in and escorted through the club, his phone was on the "Go Live" Facebook app. Everyone who was watching him "Go Live" watched as he had two expensive bottles delivered to his table, a table that he had all to his lonesome. He had several Facebook famous male and females come up to him and give him fake dap and hugs. The women wanted him because of his fame and celebrity. The men didn't like him because he was a threat to their relationships. They just acknowledged him when they ran into him because they didn't want to be exposed as haters. Mario was inside one of Orlando's biggest, hottest clubs, walking around making the party scene all about himself. He didn't drink, smoke, or dance. The expensive champagne he ordered just sat there like a expensive table ornament. He had just come to the club to film his ride to the club, his entrance into the club, and his exit which he was now filming. He walked back outside, back near the front entrance where all the people in the long line to get into the club could see him. He had one of Tony Glover's security team go and have the limo driver pick him up in the front, out where everyone could witness his departure. He got in the back of the limo and was proud of the show he had just put on for his audience of his very own Reality T.V. show. Then all of a sudden the "Likes" "Comments," and "Pokes" started piling in on his Facebook account.

Shanell

Shanell was on Facebook looking through all of the pictures she had downloaded to her page over the years. She really, really missed her only child, and felt quite lonely without her. They would usually be sitting around talking like best friends, sort of like a big sister, little sister thing. Whenever they got bored with sitting around the house they would go mall hopping, to the movies, or to pick up one of Maddy's many friend girls. Shanell had a few friends her own age, but the problem she had with them was they all acted their age. She preferred hanging around Maddy and her friends in her age group. They helped her feel young, sexy, and carefree all over again. At 39 years old, Shanell still had a nice slim sexy shape, one that most women her age who had borne several children didn't have anymore. She preferred to wear the clothing of the younger generation as well, as opposed to the safe sophisticated look the women her age preferred.

Now that Maddy was away at school in Tallahassee, Shanell was really beginning to feel lonely. Domonique had been incarcerated for the past 15 years and he was the only man that she had ever been with sexually in her entire life. When he was locked up at Coleman Medium Federal prison in Wildwood, Florida, she would go up and see him all the time. A couple of times when she didn't have Maddy with her, they were able to sneak and get a quickie in. But she hadn't been able to see him, touch him, kiss him, or sneak and get a quickie in with him for the past 18 months since they moved him to USP Florence way out in Florence, Colorado. He had been transferred because he got caught up in a riot where another inmate was killed, and a guard trying to break it up was accidentally stabbed and paralyzed. Domonique was not guilty of stabbing the inmate or the guard, but he was charged with inciting rioting with a whole bunch of other inmates. That charge raised his custody level, and they shipped him out of Coleman so fast he wasn't able to tell family and friends he was being moved. They kept him in transition so much that it took his mail two to three months to catch up with him whenever someone wrote him or sent him money. He didn't hear from Shanell or Maddy for 11 months, because he was in transition so much. Shanell and Maddy were beginning to get worried about him as well, so after five months of not hearing from him, and getting some of his mail sent back to them, they finally called Coleman Medium and were informed that he had been involved in a riot and shipped to an undisclosed place. They were told that the Federal Bureau of Prisons did not and would not announce an inmate's location while he was being transported. They were told that they would have to wait until Domonique made it to his designated prison, and he would have to contact them and disclose all of his information to them.

Shanell really missed him, not just because of the sex that they snuck and had from time to time. But she was lonely without him and Maddy. For the first time she was all alone, without having at least one of them there for her. She also missed a man's touch, attention, and affection. Domonique provided her with all of these things when she went to visitation. He would hold her hands during the visits, caress her arms, and look her in her eyes when he talked to her. As she sat there reminiscing at the pictures she had downloaded on her Facebook page, she noticed something strange. Someone had just "Poked" her. She was confused. "What did this mean?" she thought.

Sonic

Superproducer Jay was getting more and more friend requests each day. Men and women alike were sending him requests. None of these people knew Sonic, or Superproducer Jay as he was calling himself. Sonic laughed at all of these dudes and thirsty chicks trying to send him friend requests and they were not even friends, or for that matter didn't even know each other. He hadn't been in Orlando long enough to get to know or meet any of these people sending him friend requests. Orlando was a 7-nights-a-week party town. It was easy to fool a town like that by going on social media, and proclaiming yourself to be a club promoter, producer, rapper or athlete. Unsuspecting, starstruck people didn't ask questions right away when you already came with a known name.

What the people who were friend-requesting Superproducer Jay didn't know was that they were being catfished by a merciless, ruthless killer who was on the hunt for his next victim. He wasn't interested in the many females that were friend-requesting "Poking" and inboxing him, thinking that he might be the big money baller that they needed in their life. He preferred lowlife women, not high-class hoes that worked and did things correctly by the book. He wanted the strippers, the tricks, the women that sold drugs, because he knew all of these women were still connected to the streets. They all preferred a fast dollar, and he knew they all could be easily convinced to help set up some dudes so that he could rob them. He was more interested in the dudes that had money—the flashy money flossers, the car and rim showers.

He studied Facebook and Instagram like a homework assignment. He couldn't understand how these people put all of their business on a social network full of people that didn't know, didn't like, and didn't truly care about them. He made up a persona, named it Superproducer Jay and all the friend requests, "Pokes," and inbox messages started pouring in as if this was a real person. Little did these unsuspecting people know that Sonic was a spider weaving his web of lies and deceptions, waiting and anticipating getting someone caught up in his sticky, strong web. Once caught up in his web the life would be slowly sucked right out of his prey.

Sonic walked over to the bed, inside of his room at the seedy Budget Motel he was staying in on Orange Blossom Trail. He started ironing his clothes that he was going to wear out today. He was getting ready to go to the Flashdancers strip club right up the street, walking distance from his room. His plan for the night was to go down to the club and bring one of those strippers he had been flirting with back to his room and pop a couple Mollys, snort some cocaine, drink some Ciroc, and get as freaky as possible. Just as it started getting dark out and the streetlights started lighting up Orange Blossom Trail, Sonic headed out to go and get his party favorites for the girl he would be bringing back to his room, and from there to Flashdancers. He would be back later to check his Facebook account and see how many more were inching towards his web.

Kei Kei

Kei Kei was sitting between her on-again, off-again, today on-again friend Ashley's legs, getting her underbraids done for her 27 piece hairdo. They were at their homegirl Jessica's house in Pheasant Run condominiums in Rosemont. They were doing what they did, best sitting around gossiping and telling war stories about the dudes they dated and the hoes they were going to fight when they saw them. They talked about photos, twerk videos, fights, and war texting that other people were involved in on Facebook and Instagram. Jessica and Kei Kei started talking about this girl named Lucy who Jessica used to be real cool with. Kei Kei told Jessica that she was going to fight Lucy because Lucy had disrespected her friend Jessica by tagging Jessica's ex/baby daddy in a post as her MCM (Man crush Monday).

Jessica told Kei Kei, "Girl, don't worry about fighting that homeless bitch Lucy, she was miserable already."

Kei Kei said, "Jessica girl, I told you these hoes ain't your friends. They all hang around you because you have your own place and your own car."

Ashley immediately stopped doing Kei Kei's underbraids and said "Hoe, I know you ain't talking about me."

Kei Kei fakely said "Naw, bitch, you are here with us. Why would I be talking about you? I'm talking about all those other hoes Jessica be having around her."

It seemed like Kei Kei was more upset and hyped by what Lucy was being accused of than Jessica who was doing the accusing. Ashley got quiet and sat there working on Kei Kei's underbraids. She got quiet because she was creeping and sleeping with her close friend Jessica's ex/baby daddy too.

As a matter of fact, Ashley and Kei Kei had a big fight that was videoed and downloaded onto Facebook and Instagram 19 days ago. It all started when one day when Kei Kei's phone was dead and she asked Ashley if she could use her phone. Ashley didn't know that Kei Kei was going to call Super Dave, the neighborhood fraud scam artist that was known also for breaking bread with the neighborhood tramps in exchange for sex. Ashley knew that he was Kei Kei's man, but Kei Kei wasn't her friend. She was the friend of her friend Jessica, so she was going to keep tricking with Super Dave behind Kei Kei's back. Kei Kei dialed Super Dave's phone number from Ashley's phone and the screen lit up and the name Super Dave appeared on the screen. Kei Kei thought that it was strange that Ashley had her man's number already programmed into her phone, but before she could say something to her about it, something stranger happened. Super Dave answered on the first ring and said "Damn I thought you ain't fuck with a nigga no more."

Kei Kei said "What?" into the phone so that she could access and make sure she was hearing the voice of her man Super Dave.

He said, "You heard me, Ashley, sometimes you be on some bullshit, girl; you been pump faking on a nigga for the past couple of weeks."

Kei Kei said, "Yeah, bae, she been pump faking on me too". She then dropped Ashley's phone and punched her square in the jaw. Ashley who was known for fighting too recovered quickly and fired back hitting Kei Kei back in her mouth. They had a weave-pulling, tittie-showing face-scratching, knock-down, drag-out battle that day.

That day when they fought, they were around at least 6 more of their so-called friends, including Jessica. But instead of these so-called friends running to break it up, they ran and grabbed their cell phones so that they could record this epic battle and post it on social media. Weeks later everyone in Rosemont, Pine Hills, Richmond Heights, Ivey Lane, Lake Mann, Carver Shores, and across town were talking about that fight, giving a blow-by-blow commentary on Ashley's titties while she and Kei Kei exchanged blows. Some said Kei Kei won, some said Ashley won, but there were many views and many comments. But here they were 19 days later, sitting here with one doing the other's hair, trusting each other at least until after this hairdo was done, just as nothing had ever happened. Kei Kei still young and immature, foolishly in love with Super Dave. Ashley still young, naïve, and sheisty, still creeping with Super Dave and any man with or without a girlfriend willing to pay her for sex. She still got with him from time to time while Kei Kei was on CEP's campus trying to get an education, and a diploma.

Jessica, the common link between both girls, knew both sides and played it to her advantage. She too had tricked with Super Dave on a couple of occasions. She felt like all of these hoes were either sleeping with or wanted to sleep with her ex/baby daddy, so she was just playing the dirty game that they had started. She sat there shooting the breeze with these hoes but she did not trust them. She sat there with her camera phone ready just in case something jumped off between these young dumb hoes. If it did, she was going to do what she did best, capture the action and download it on Facebook, Instagram or maybe even World Star Hip Hop.

Mario

Mario's cell phone was blowing up, ringing every 3 or 4 minutes. He knew who it was. It was Tina trying to get taken back to the Geneva Hotel for another round of sex with semi-celebrity Mario. She had called, texted, poked, inboxed, and instant messaged him for the past 2 hours, and he never responded to any of her attempts to reach him. Another text message came through his phone saying that she wanted a refill of what he had given her a week ago. She was sending emojis and sexually explicit pictures to his inbox. She even left a message on his wall that he quickly deleted. He saw all of her desperate attempts to reach him and kept right on doing what he was doing. He enjoyed making these thirsty females sweat him and wait for his call or answer. He was going to get with Tina again. He liked how she did whatever he asked of her sexually. Another call from Tina, another text, another emoji, another Poke.

Mario saw them all, but he was online viewing Tina's best friend and running buddy Slimbaby Kia's profile pictures. She too had poked him and left him explicit pictures and messages inside his inbox. He was viewing her profile pictures to see how she looked. She was slim, fine, and sexy as hell, just like Mario liked them. She knew that her friend and running mate Tina liked this guy and was sleeping with him on the side, but Tina had broken the golden rule by telling Kia how good this man Mario was in bed. Plus Kia knew that Tina had a fiancé, so she couldn't raise no hell about a nigga that wasn't her man. Mario knew that both of these hoes had fiances. It clearly said it on both their Facebook and Instagram pages, and the both of them had several photos with these men. But here the both of them were, blowing up his inbox and cell phone and willing to give him the kind of time, attention, and sex that they should only be willing to give the men that held the fiance titles. He labeled them as "Fame Whores" who sought after friendships, relationships, and situationships with men and women that had huge followings on Facebook, Instagram, and other well-known social media sites.

Just like Tina, Kia had a fiance too, but she was in hot pursuit chasing behind someone else's man just like millions of other women were doing on these Social media sites. Tina and Kia were best friends, both of them were engaged to two first cousins. Tina was engaged to Randy, and Kia was engaged to Efrem. Randy had introduced his cousin to Kia and they had been a couple ever since. At this very moment while Randy and Efrem were away at a family reunion out of town, their brides to be were in a Facebook famous dude's inbox, offering him sexual favors and pornographic sex with no strings attached. Another text message came through from Tina, "Are you ignoring me"?

Mario texted her back. "I will call you back later, I'm with my lady" he lied.

Tina, unfazed and unconcerned with Mario's lady, texted back " Okay, hurry up, my nigga is out of town and I want a refill."

Mario laughed out loud at her thirstiness, and went right back to having an inbox conversation with her best friend Slimbaby Kia. Two hours later, he and Slimbaby Kia were in a hotel room in Daytona Beach doing all the things they said that they would do to each other in their inbox conversations. Slimbaby Kia was even better and freakier than Tina. She was flexible, she was nimble, she was willing, and she was a super freak. She was putting on a show for Mario's hidden camera and she didn't even know it. If and when this tape ever got out, Slimbaby Kia would get rave reviews for the performance she was putting on. Mario really liked her. He laid and pillow-talked with her afterwards, telling her the business of many dudes who he was dealing with and fronting drugs to. Then her phone rang and she looked at the screen and made the shhhh sign with her fingers and mouth to let Mario know that it was her fiance. She got her naked, fine, slim, sexy self out of the bed of sins she had just created with Mario and walked over near the bathroom and talked to her fiance Efrem. She talked to him as if he were the only man for her, and the love of her life. She talked to him with so much love and respect. Mario thought to himself "This bitch ain't shit, but she's good. Where was all of this love and respect twenty minutes ago when she was sexing me out of that same mouth that she talking sweet love stories to him with now?"

His phone rang. He looked down at the screen—it was Tina again. He motioned for Slimbaby Kia to come back over and finish her conversation, because he needed to get in the bathroom. She did, and he went inside the bathroom and closed the door behind him. He turned the water on in the shower and began talking to Tina. He said, "Yo, Tina, what's up?

Mario lied to her and told her that he was out of town with his lady on an unexpected trip, and that he would make sure to get with her tomorrow. That was good enough for her, she agreed to it, and they hung up. He went back out into the room where fine ass Slimbaby Kia was still standing there naked, lying to Efrem on the phone. She made eye contact with Mario, then walked over and lay across the bed of sins they had performed their lustful acts on. She motioned to him with her mouth and two fingers that she wanted a round two. Mario smiled thinking to himself that he had another satisfied customer. While still on the phone with her fiance, Kia got up off the bed and walked over to Mario and started stroking his flaccid manhood. A few strokes followed by a few kisses had him back ready in a matter of minutes. That was when Kia told Efrem she would call him back later. She hung up the phone and climbed on top of Mario and finished re-enacting some of the things she bragged about she was going to do to him in his inbox. All the while, the unblinking eye just kept rolling and collecting video footage.

Shanell

Shanell was up at one of her and Maddy's favorite places, Goff's Ice Cream shop. While she was standing in line waiting on them to prepare the banana milk shake that she had ordered, she noticed a whole bunch of flyers of a local rapper named K.T. As she stepped out of line to go and get a closer look at the flyers, she noticed that the flyers were on a marquee for an up and coming show he was performing at a club called The Barn down in Sanford, Florida. K.T. and another hot up-and-coming rapper from Orlando named Tonii Boi were performing next weekend at The Barn. She knew right then and there that she was going to be in that crowd at The Barn next weekend. She knew that Lil boy K.T. She was close friends with his Auntie Bell. She watched him grow up and attend some of the same elementary and middle schools that Maddy attended. She hadn't seen him in a while, ever since his mom Bell's big sister Mesha moved away. But now K.T. was back a grown man and an up-and-coming rap star. She was going to go and support him, but more importantly she was going to get out of the house and do something. She hadn't really been anywhere or done much since Maddy touched down in Tallahassee.

She went home and went online and ordered her ticket to K.T. and Tonii Boi's show. Then she logged on Instagram to check her account and everyone was talking about the show next weekend. Then she checked her Facebook page and there she spotted it

41

again, some guy that she didn't know had "poked" her again. She still didn't know what a "poke" meant, so she reached for her cell phone to call the one person who had always guided and advised her through this social media mess, Maddy.

It was quite funny to Maddy that someone had actually "poked" her Mama, and was interested in her in that way. After all her 39-year-old Mama had never dealt with another man in all her life, besides her father Domonique. Maddy had mixed emotions about this situation though. Although it was a little funny at first, the more she thought about it, she knew her mom was there in Orlando all by herself. She could be a sitting duck to any of the internet thugs, frauds, and catfishers from anywhere in the world. She wasn't there to help guide her mom away from the internet predators. She was happy for her mom in that someone was showing interest in her in that way. She knew the situation firsthand about her mother being lonely without the only man that had ever touched her body, her father. But on the other hand she was loyal to her dad, in that she would never fully approve anyone to take his place. She explained to Shanell what getting a "poke" symbolized. She warned her mom to be very careful, that there were characters hiding in the shadows all the way around the world that got on Facebook and Instagram. In this new Internet, social media world, the kids taught the parents about the dangers of social media.

Sonic

Sonic was walking back from the Quick Stop on Kaley and Orange Blossom Trail, coming from getting more blunts and bottled water for him and Shay, one of the strippers from Flashdancers. They had been up all night snorting coke, popping Mollys, smoking dirty weed joints called "Boonk," and having pornographic sex. Shay wasn't the cutest female from Flashdancer's, but she was down for whatever. She always wore lacefront wigs and a lot of makeup, but she had a banging body of a perfect 10 proportions. She had a high sex drive and hardly ever said no or stop. That was what Sonic liked about her. He walked back to his room at the Budget Motel, put his key in the door, and walked into the unlit, one-bed room. Shay didn't move a muscle. He reached and turned on the lamp and saw her stretch-markless, fine, perfect, naked body lying on the bed. Then all of a sudden she turned over and he thought he was looking into the face of a booger bear, or maybe even or more accurately a clown without its make-up on. Her lacefront wig had fallen off, possibly last night when they were having the rough sex that they both preferred. And at this very moment Sonic wasn't sure if a transexual had snuck in his room and replaced the fine-ass stripper that had come to his room with him last night. Shay had no edges; scars, bumps and craters marred her face. Just then Sonic realized why lacefront wigs and makeup were both a part of her daily uniform package. She smiled with only a face a mother could love pained smile, and Sonic quickly turned the lights back off.

Sonic said, "Sorry, I didn't mean to wake you," but what he really was thinking was he didn't want to face her.

He walked over to his laptop sitting on the table in the room and logged on to his Facebook account. His made-up persona Superproducer Jay had received a lot more friend requests, "pokes" and inbox messages. One of the friend requests stood out in particular. It was one from this flashy flamboyant dude named Mario. He had friend requested Sonic and sent him an inbox message saying. "Yo player, I notice King shit when I see it, since the both of us Kings. That means we're both from royalty. I got a plan to bring Lil Wayne and Drake to town in concert and I need you, being the quality Superproducer and Club Promoter that you are, to team up with me so that we can get this money. Hit me back up and let me know your level of interest. King."

Sonic started viewing Mario's Facebook profile and knew that this was who he was looking for to rob. This dude's life, lifestyle, and business was an open book to Sonic. Sonic wondered why would a guy, legit or illegal, divulge all of his personal and private business to people he barely knew, for anyone to view.

Someway, somehow, Shay appeared out of nowhere and started rubbing on him in a sexual way. Even though it was dark in the room, the image of her without her lacefront wig on a few minutes ago was still fresh in his head. There was no way he could have sex with her now without being high, drunk, or both. He accepted Mario's friend request. He then pulled out the Mollys he had walked up OBT and bought earlier. He popped one in his mouth and put one up to Shay's mouth. She opened it, he shoved one in her mouth, and she swallowed it. Then he took a sip of the bottled water that he bought also and gave Shay a sip. He turned back to Mario's Facebook page, viewing all of his world that he allowed the rest of the world access to. Three minutes later the anti-depressant started to kick in. He walked over to the edge of the bed in his room, took his pants off, and allowed Shay to do what she did best. Things began to slow down for him. He was wide awake but he felt as if he were sleep walking. He sat there on the edge of the bed as that sexy beast Shay gave him oral pleasure. He looked down at her as her head bobbed up and down. The full effect of the Molly was now flowing through his blood stream. In this very moment while inebriated on a Molly, Sonic thought Shay didn't look so bad with her lacefront wig off.

Kei Kei

Kei Kei was doing really, really well in school at CEP. She had gotten caught back up on all of her school work that she fell behind on. Her GPA was an eye popping 3.8. She was spending a lot of quality time with her son Prince. She was home before curfew, and doing everything she was supposed to with her probation. Her Probation Officer Mrs. Washington even informed her that if she could keep up the good progress for another 6 months, she would put in for her sentencing judge to give her early termination. She hadn't had a fight in 3 months, finished her community service hours, and raised her GPA.

The only negative thing going on in her life at the moment was that her relationship with Super Dave was on the outs. Super Dave wasn't calling, texting, or coming around like they were together still. She found herself having to "Poke," inbox, and text him just like the rest of the thirsty hoes had to. Her frustrations got so bad that she took them to social media by making statuses about no good niggas and tagging Super Dave's name in most of them. Still no call or response from Super Dave. Kei Kei was about ready to snap. She started back getting into long heated arguments with females on Facebook who commented on those angry statuses she posted. There were several screen shots and war texts that went on for weeks.

Her arguments started getting so intense other people began to chime in. There were threats of "Pull up, hoe," "I ain't doing no talking when I see that that hoe,"and "I'm popping off on sight." There were so many people involved in this post war that some found themselves arguing with people that they were kin to, all because so many had commented and put their opinion in Kei Kei's post. The next thing you know Jessica was telling Lucy to meet her at Rosemont Park so that they could square up. Lucy's friend Simone then chimed in "Y'all hoes kill me with this fake loyalty shit, all y'all hoes having sex with each other's nigga". And" Y'all ain't jumping my friend Lucy either."

Then Kei Kei said "Well, y'all hoes link up together and come and meet us at Rosemont park then, scary ass bitches."

Ashley chimed in, "Ain't nobody gonna fuck with my dawgs, Jessica or Kei Kei. Y'all hoes just running your suck muscles."

They argued, war texted, and sent embarrassing videos and pictures of each other for several days. But no one ever pulled up on the other, or met up in designated places. Several people blocked each other; several people unfriended and unfollowed others. After all of that Kei Kei still hadn't heard from or seen Super Dave.

Mario

The camera was rolling, but this time Mario the video-hiding voyeur, was being videoed without his knowledge, consent, or approval. He was down at one of the places he used as a front for one of the fake businesses he ran. He was at his fledgling trucking company, which was currently under surveillance by DEA agents that had been following the man Mario was standing talking with down at the truck yard. The DEA had followed this man through 4 states: Texas, Louisiana, Georgia and now Florida. Parked across the street filming these two men at this little small remote truck yard, they were wondering just who the guy was that the truck driver meeting with. Mario and the trucker talked for a few minutes and then they both walked inside the small portable building that was used as office headquarters for the trucking company. Thirty minutes later with the surveillance camera still rolling, Mario and the trucker came walking back outside. The driver walked up to his 18-wheel rig, pulled four heavily duct-taped packages from an underneath hidden compartment, and handed them to Mario. The DEA agents had already called for extra surveillance just in case. When these two suspects went in opposite directions, they could put a tail on both of them. Mario then went inside his SUV and came back out with a black leather satchel and handed it to the trucker. The trucker looked inside the satchel, checked the contents inside, reached his hand out and shook Mario's, and then turned on his heels and headed back to his rig. He cranked his 18-wheel monster up and slowly made his way back out into traffic, all with two nearly invisible, undistinguishable DEA agents in an unmarked car following him and filming his every move. The other car that was dispatched earlier as backup remained behind with two more DEA officers sitting in an unmarked car out of view across the street from the truck yard. They were assigned to follow the new unknown fellow that the 18-wheel trucker had just secretly met up with and exchanged suspicious packages with. The man who liked to secretly record and videotape unsuspecting women was now being secretly recorded and videotaped himself. The man who always wanted to star in his own Reality T.V. show was performing live in a DEA version of must-see T.V. Soon and very soon they planned on taking down this self-proclaimed star.

Shanell

Shanell's father was in town. He had called her earlier and said that he had just crossed the Georgia line and was in North Florida, headed down to Orlando with a drop off. He told her that he wanted to go and sit down and have a bite to eat with her while he was in town. She told him about a new restaurant in Orlando run by a little entreprenurial chick called Rell's Kitchen and asked him to call her when he was coming through the Deland-Deltona area, because all she had to do was call Rell on her cellphone and she would deliver within 30 minutes. She then heard a familiar ping come from her cellphone Facebook account. She hung up with her dad and swiped her screen to get to her Facebook page. It was the same dude who had "poked" her the two times before; he had just "poked" her again.

Now that Maddy had explained to her just what "poking" was and meant, she was going check out this dude's (whose profile name was BA Boutthatlyfe) pictures and statuses. It said that he was 33, single, no kids. He lived in Orlando, but was originally from Columbia, Missouri. He was mad handsome and sexy, he was high yellow with a bunch of tattoos and long flowing dreadlocks. He had gold fronts on his teeth, with eye brows that had parts cut in them, and several tattoos on his face. This man was totally thugged out, and it turned Shanell on. So she did something that she herself didn't expect, she "poked" him back. She continued to go through BA Boutthatlyfe's pictures to see if she could find out more about him. She wanted to see if they had any mutual friends, but they didn't have any. Then she went on his timeline to see where he had grown up, attended high school, or worked. To her surprise all of these were left blank. Now Shanell was even more confused by this sexy yella fella. She had done all of the protocols that Maddy had instructed her to do, and still came up with unanswered questions.

A moment later she was brought back to reality by her phone ringing. It was her dad telling her to call and order the food. He was passing through Orange City which was 15-20 minutes away. She asked him what he wanted to eat, and he asked her what was on the menu. She told him about Rell's famous Hoobachi that she made up several different ways and delivered to you hot and steaming. He agreed to get it with his favorite shrimps in it and they hung up. Her thoughts went back to that sexy-ass man BA Boutthatlyfe. She wondered why she was so interested in him, and why he had so much interest in her. He "poked" her back again. She wasn't about to play the "poke" game all day with him. She inboxed him and said, "If you keep 'poking' me I'm going to end up pregnant LOL. If you're interested in hollering at me, I'm leaving my cellphone number in your inbox. Call me tonight at 9."

Sonic

Superproducer Jay was almost up to 5000 followers and the friend requests just kept coming in. Sonic loved this Facebook and Instagram phenomenon; they had become his wing man in fooling these flossing ass dudes. Social media had become just like casing a bank, all you had to do was sit back and watch as these men and women put all of their business on display. So he watched Facebook and Instagram, he studied them, and he learned all he could about the people he was aiming to rob. A lot of these people were more brazen and flamboyant than others when it came to posting their personal business. Others he felt should have just put a big X on their own back, or gone to the local police station and attempted to turn themselves in, because they were doing so much a case or indictment was sure to come anytime soon. These fools posted their whereabouts, every time they went out of town, or to the Mall. They posted their feelings, like when they were bored. When they were horny they would post a pornographic picture and caption it with Mood! If they hit their number in Lotto or a scratch off they would screenshot a picture of their winning ticket. And now that they had this new "Go Live" app many of them wanted attention so bad they went live more than they would post statuses. He thanked whoever came up with the idea of Facebook, Instagram and social media. Whoever invented these allowed him to remain behind the shadows and stalk his victims from the comfort of his own home.

Sonic noticed that Orlando was much like his hometown of Detroit, Michigan. They both were high crime, low income major cities, that were drug riddled and prostitution laden. He fit in and blended in well in Orlando. He clicked onto Mario's Facebook page. He watched the video that Mario had gone live on when he took the limousine to the club. He was studying that Mario dude; he was an open book test that Sonic was going to ace. Mario and all the rest of these characters deserved what he was planning on doing to them, he thought.

Facebook and Instagram had become a runway of models that showed way more of themselves than what people needed to see. It seemed as if everyone on there was trying to outdo each other. Robbers such as Sonic were the talent agents that the flossers were modeling for. He watched as Mario walked out and got into the stretch limo, pulled away from the curb in front of his house, left his gated community, and then at the club. He kept rewinding and viewing the video several times. He was looking for a clue, a mistake by Mario that would get Sonic one step closer to robbing this dude. He spotted it. There it was, what might end up being Mario's fatal flaw. He rewound to where Mario first walked out of the front door to his house, stepped off of his front porch, and walked down the front sidewalk in front of his house to the limo. Just as he threw up the deuces sign he flashed past his mailbox. Right there on his mailbox was his address. Sonic wrote down the 4-digit number and started working on finding out where Mario laid his head.

Kei Kei

Kei Kei was coming up Old Winter Garden road about to make a right turn on Ivey Lane. She was playing it awfully close to breaking curfew. She was riding in the car with Jessica and Ashley who had both texted her 30 minutes ago and told her the rumor that they had heard about her man Super Dave. Ashley told her that she had heard that he was dating a high yellow girl that lived in Lake Mann Gardens apartments. Then Jessica called saying that she heard that the high yellow girl was pregnant by Super Dave. Kei Kei's mind raced a mile a minute; she couldn't understand why he would disrespect her in this manner. They turned into the entrance to Lake Mann Gardens. When you entered this complex you could go only to the left, or to the right. Once you made your choice of direction to go, all you could do was drive to the back of the complex and turn around and come all the way back up front to go back out, because it was one way in and one way out. They went left and drove hoping to spot Super Dave or his silver Dodge Charger rental car. They drove all the way to the back of the right side of Lake Mann Gardens, but they didn't spot him or the car. They turned around in the last parking lot and drove all the way back around to the front entrance. They passed by the entrance and the front office and drove down the left side of the apartment complex. Looking for him or the car again they drove all the way to the back of the left hand side of Lake Mann Gardens. They spotted neither.

Despite getting closer with each passing minute to being in violation of her curfew, Kei Kei asked Jessica to pull the car over so that she could survey the landscape a little longer. This was insane for her to be just sitting here stalking and searching for a man who refused to answer her calls, texts, inboxes, pokes, or just pick up his phone and call her. They had a son together. The least he could do was call and check on his seed, she thought.

This was perfectly fine with Jessica; she had driven Kei Kei over here because she loved drama. She had her camera phone ready just in case, because she loved filming drama even better. Drama fueled her life as she was always looking for the chance to record someone fighting, arguing, or sexing. She was not here to support or console her young friend Kei Kei. She was here to record, download, and post her business all over Facebook, Instagram and other up-and-coming social media outlets so that she could get "Likes", comments and more followers.

Ashley was there because she was mad at Super Dave for cheating on Kei Kei and her with this new yellow hoe. He had been ignoring her calls too. He hadn't accepted a call or text from her since the last time Kei Kei called him from her phone. Twenty-two more minutes and Kei Kei would be out past curfew, but she was still sitting in the parking lot of an apartment complex that wasn't on her side of town. If she left right now she would make it with no problem, but with her sitting, letting precious minutes slip away, she was asking for trouble. With the way that traffic was unpredictable on Old Winter Garden Road and Pine Hills road, she had best leave now. She had 17 minutes left to get home. Kei Kei was going to be facing a violation of probation charge if she were late for curfew again, and 3 years of incarceration. But she just kept sitting there in a car with two women that secretly despised her. With 14 minutes left, her phone rang.

Mario

Mario had the top down on his 71' Cheverolet Chevell with the candy paint and 26' inch rims. He called himself creeping, but with that attention-calling car he was making a bunch of heads turn instead. He drove up not-so-busy Clarcona Road, quickly turned into the back entrance of the Burger King at the corner of OBT and Clarcona, parked and got out. He put the top up on his convertible, pressed the remote on his expensive security system he had installed on his car, and then turned on his heels and started walking towards the front entrance to the Burger King.

Not far behind him two men in an unmarked car pulled into the Jamaican restaurant right next to the Burger King called A Taste of Jamaica. They sat there in the parking lot and kept a close watchful eye on Mario. Mario walked past the entrance and kept walking till he got to the busy OBT traffic. He then ran across the street to a motel the agents knew as Geneva. Mario walked up to room #8, knocked, and someone opened the door and he entered. A big smile appeared on his face as he closed the door behind him. Sitting on the bed naked and waiting on him were two cousins' fiancees, Tina and Slimbaby Kia. Kia patted the bed, motioning for Mario to take off his clothes and come and join them.

Already there watching was a car with two men sitting in it, inconspicuously parked on the other end of the Geneva Motel, watching room #8.

The two DEA agents were assigned to watching Mario, hoping to video him during any kind of drug activity, pickup or delivery. They were on to him after he exchanged packages with a known big-time drug trafficker, whom they had been watching and following for two years. They were also watching and following Mario's Facebook, Instagram and social media accounts, and what they saw on there piqued their interest in him even more. This guy claimed to have all of these business ventures and after the feds checked all his tax ID numbers, they didn't add up or make sense so they alerted the IRS, and now he was being secretly investigated by two different sets of the alphabet boys. He hadn't filed taxes on any of these fake businesses that he bragged about on social media, and from the things they saw him post on his page, they knew that they were on to a major player in the game.

The two dudes parked in the Geneva motel parking lot were two cousins who were engaged to the two women who were already in room #8 where some strange dude that they didn't know had just entered. Efrem and Randy looked at each other with astonishment, as if they both were thinking "What the hell is going on?"

Then Randy said, "Why in God's name are we sitting at a seedy motel watching a man walk into a room that we saw our fiancees check into an hour ago?"

The DEA agents were following Mario. The cousins Efrem and Randy were following their fiancees Tina and Kia. But the DEA agents didn't notice the cousins, and the cousins didn't notice the DEA agents. Kia and Tina didn't notice their fiances in the nearby Geneva Motel parking lot, nor did they notice the DEA agents parked across the street watching Mario. Mario didn't notice either set of men either, but all eyes were on him. He didn't know it but he had stepped into two separate piles of shit.

Efrem, the hothead of the two, wanted to go and knock on the door to get to the bottom of what was going on inside room #8, but Randy the thinker wanted to sit and gather more evidence. Fourty-five minutes later, eight eyes were still glued to room #8 at the Geneva Motel. Inside room #8, the camera on Mario's camera phone which he had set up on top of the motel room mini fridge was recording as one man had two women that were fiancees doing things to him that a woman should only be doing with her husband. These women that were engaged to two cousins were putting their mouths and tongues in places that no one would believe if Mario hadn't recorded it. A fly on the wall trying to tell this story would have been called a liar, but a camera spoke truth and never blinked. If and when these videos got out, Tina and Slimbaby Kia would be exposed as off the chain freaks who had no limitations sexually. Efrem and Randy would soon find out that the same mouth you tell the truth out of, is the same one you tell lies from as well. These two women in room #8 at a seedy pay-per-hour motel were performing sex acts on a man they barely knew. These two women had told the cousins that they loved them, wanted to be with them forever, that they wanted to marry them, and would never betray them or hurt them. The camera kept recording, as the two women that had fiances that were first cousins kept unknowingly performing for it.

Shanell

Shanell and her dad was sitting kicking it and finishing off their delicious hot meal from Rell's Kitchen. Rell had pulled up and jumped out with their Hoobachi dinners just as her father pulled into Shanell's complex. He hopped out of his rig and walked up to Shanell's apartment as she stood there talking with Rell. Shanell introduced her dad to the short, fine, bubbly, and smiling Rell. Shanell reached into her pocket to get the money to pay her for the food that she had delivered, when her dad told her to put her money back in her pocket, he was paying for it. He reached into a black leather satchel and pulled out two $20 dollar bills, and Rell told him that he only owed her $20 dollars. He told her that the other $20 dollars were her tip, and she smiled a big toothy grin and told Shanell, "Girl, I like him already." She then gave both of them a hug, told them to enjoy their food, and then she went and jumped into her white Hyundai and sped off to her next delivery.

Shanell's dad said, "I like your friend. She got a hustle about herself."

Shanell replied, "Daddy, that young girl will make your old self throw a rod trying to keep up with her."

He said "Don't underestimate your old boy. I handle that big girl out there in the parking lot every day and she's way bigger than your lil friend."

Shanell couldn't do anything but laugh at what her Pops had just said. They sat there and caught up on old times for over an hour before her father said that he needed to get back on the road. He reached inside the black satchel and handed her $2500 dollars cash money. He told her to pay her rent for the next two months and send his granddaughter Maddy the other $1000 dollars. He told her that he loved her and had to get back on the road. He told her to tell Maddy to call him, he hugged his daughter tightly, and then headed back to his 18-wheel girlfriend.

After he left, Shanell cleaned up from where she and her father had eaten the wonderful Hoobachi from Rell's Kitchen, then she walked out to her car to go and Western Union Maddy the money her grandfather had left for her. She texted Maddy the confirmation number for her wire transfer, and all the rest of the information that she would need in order for her to go and pick her money up, and then she returned home.

When Shanell walked into her apartment she logged on to her Facebook page and noticed that not only had BA Boutthatlyfe "poked" her again, but he had friend requested her, and left his cell phone number. She quickly accepted his friend request and laid down to take a much-needed nap, before she would wake up and give BA a call. Two hours later she was awakened by ping after ping on her inbox on her Facebook page. BA Boutthatlyfe was blowing up her inbox with emojis and messages. He had even left a few messages on her wall, after Shanell had accepted his friend request. "Hey sexy, thanks for the add." "You gonna let me be your little friend?" "Just give a nigga like me a chance." All this new attention was making Shanell tingle inside, and smile outside. She went to go and view this sexy ass man's profile again, Damn this couldn't be real, she thought to herself. This man was cute and sexy, and he was interested in her. She started typing back into his inbox, "About to call you right now."

Sonic

Sonic wasn't from Orlando, he was from Detroit, but he sure did find his way around town well. He and Shay were riding through Windermere following the guidance of the GPS. They had typed in Mario's 4 digit numbers that were on his mailbox. Sonic was running low on cash, the money that he was spending weekly at the Budget Motel for his room was taking a toll on the $5000 dollars the city of Detroit had paid him to leave. He was intent on finding this flossing, showboating nigga named Mario, and lighting his ass on fire.

Sonic had no mercy on his victims; he hated and despised flossers. He didn't feel sorry for them when they begged him for their life. The very first guy that he had ever robbed at the age of 14 was a guy named Mike Adams. Mike always cracked jokes on Sonic and made fun of his clothes and lack of style in front of everybody. Sonic came from a poor single parent home, while Mike's mother was a well-known stripper and his father was a big-time drug dealer. Mike Adams wore all the latest styles all throughout elementary, middle, and high school. He made fun of Sonic and a lot of the other kids who were not as fortunate as he was. Over the years Sonic grew tired of his actions and his mouth, and secretly swore to shut him up someday. That day came in both of their freshman year at Detroit King High. They were at their school bus stop waiting for the bus to come and pick them up early one morning when Mike started in on him because Sonic was wearing a pair of Stephon Marbury's $15 dollar shoes and he had on the new Jordan 11's. Waiting for Mike to start something, Sonic had stolen a gun out of a car he had burglarized a week earlier. Sonic pulled the gun out on Mike Adams at the school bus stop and robbed him in front of everybody, making him strip down to his boxers. He even made him take off his Jordans, although Mike wore a size 11 and Sonic only wore a size 9. He told Mike to take off walking after he had made him strip off his clothes and shoes. Then to add insult to injury, he shot him in his right butt cheek to really teach him a lesson about messing with him.

After that he became feared and a living legend amongst the streets of Detroit as someone not to mess with. The next day when the police arrived at King High to arrest him on aggravated assault charges, he was wearing the Jordans that he had shot Mike Adams in the ass over, and that were two sizes too big for his feet.

Now he was planning on making an example of Mario with his flashy flossing ass, for all of Orlando to see. The GPS led him and Shay to the front gate of a gated community. There were armed guards at the entrance of the gated community that were ID'ing visitors trying to gain entrance. Sonic and Shay quickly did a U-turn and got out of the line. But they now knew where Mario lived. All they had to do was find a way to get inside without the guards ID'ing them. They were going to pay him an unexpected, uninvited visit. Sort of like a surprise party with ski masks and all. They turned around and headed back to the Budget Motel on OBT, where they had Mollys and Ciroc waiting on them. Mario didn't know it yet but he was going to be paying Sonic's rent up for months there at his room real soon. Plus with all that money, jewelry and cars that he flossed on Facebook, Mario was going to be making a sizeable donation to Sonic's drugs and party lifestyle.

Kei Kei

Sitting on the wrong side of town, in the wrong neighborhood, inside of a car with two chicks that didn't truly have her best interest at heart, instead of being home with her son and Mom, making curfew, 16-year-old Kei Kei was only 13 minutes away from violating probation and being sent away until her 19th birthday. Jessica nor Ashley were advising her to drop her witchhunt for Super Dave and make it home before she broke curfew. She was in the presence of two different shades of fake friends. Jessica wanted to see her embroiled in drama so that she could video it, and Ashley wanted the no-good man she was searching for and about to break curfew for.

Then all of a sudden her phone rang. She looked down at her screen expecting for it to be her Mama Tanya calling to see if she were near or on her way home, but to her surprise the screen said "Bae." It was Super Dave.

She quickly answered, and to her surprise Super Dave came on her line speaking loudly and angrily. He said, "Kei Kei, where you at?" He had some nerve. 12 minutes left.

Kei Kei said, "Nigga, where you at? And where the hell have you been? I've been calling, texting, emailing, inboxing you, and riding by your house and you got the nerve to be calling my phone all loud and mad and questioning me. You act like you ain't got no lady and child out here."

He said, "Yeah, Bae, I'm gonna tell you about what happened and why I ain't been able to get back at you when I see you, but where you at though?"

"I'm on my way home, trying to get there before I break curfew and have Ms. Washington all up in my ass." While she was talking to Super Dave, she was motioning for Jessica to crank up the car and drive off. She lied and said "I was helping Jessica do Ashley's pinch plaits but we're on our way to my house now."

Super Dave knew that this was a lie, because he was right there in Lake Mann Gardens looking at Kei Kei, Jessica, and cross action ass Ashley from an upstairs apartment. While they were riding through the apartment complex looking for Super Dave, they passed right by his partner Teddy as he was coming back into the apartment complex with one of the two pretty high yellow sisters that he and Super Dave were talking to and visiting in Lake Mann Gardens. Kei Kei, Jessica, and Ashley didn't see Teddy and the girl because they were looking so hard for Super Dave or his silver Dodge Charger rental car. But Teddy, who went by the name Teddy Hawk, because he was known for being able to spot trouble, the police, or a lick from far off, spotted them and quickly called Super Dave and let him know that Kei Kei and them hoes Jessica and Ashley were in Lake Mann Gardens riding around.

After Super Dave watched them pass Otisha's apartment, he came out on her balcony stoop and crouched down and was watching them dumb ass hoes ride around circling the entire apartment complex. He went outside so that Otisha couldn't hear his conversation with Kei Kei. After he knew Kei Kei was headed back home he went back inside where his new boo Otisha was sitting there smoking a blunt and talking to her sister La'tima and Teddy. Super Dave was really into Otisha. She had his nose wide open the moment that he had seen her sitting up under her mom's carport on North Lane down near Meadowbrook Middle. Otisha was what most men considered a redbone dime piece, she was fine as wine, and above all she was an independent woman. She had her own car, her own apartment, and her own hustle. Super Dave's money and street status didn't impress her; it was his swagger that got her attention. She always did prefer men with a quiet style and confidence over the flossing attention seekers. Her dad Otis, who had died a few years earlier from an unjustified police shooting, had instilled in his daughters Otisha and La'tima that although they were beautiful, they needed to bring something to the table other than their looks. Her first boyfriend had cheated on her with a girl that didn't look half as good or finer than her, but the girl had a job, a bank account, and wore the best weave and clothes though. After that, Otisha got her own money from her hustle of boosting clothes. She dumped the dude and was a free agent for the last two years. Her little sister La'tima was a spitting image of her, but slightly slimmer.

Super Dave had lied to Kei Kei and told her that he was on the 408 coming from the eastside, handling some business, and was headed to her house to see their son Prince. Five minutes left before curfew violation. Jessica was flying down Pine Hills Road running yellow and red lights, trying to help Kei Kei make curfew. Since there wasn't going to be any drama to film, she figured she'd get the young girl home so that she wouldn't violate and get locked up. They made it to the major intersection of Pine Hills Road and Silver Star right near Kei Kei's old school Evans High, and she blew through that intersection with three minutes left to get Kei Kei home. All they needed was for the next light not to be red and they had a chance to get Kei Kei there in time. As they quickly approached Indian Hill Road there was no cars there and the light was green. They turned onto Indian Hill Road and pulled in front of Kei Kei's house with a minute to spare. She hopped out and thanked Jessica and Ashley for getting her home in time, told them she would call them later on in the week, and then headed for her front door. The drama queens backed out of her driveway, turned left on to Indian Hill Road headed towards Powers Drive, and disappeared. Just as Kei Kei grabbed the door knob and walked into her home, someone was pulling into the same driveway that Jessica and Ashley had pulled out of a moment earlier. She thought that it might be Super Dave because he had just called and said he was coming to see her and Prince. She looked back to get a better view and spotted Mrs. Washington getting out of her state-issued unmarked car.

Mario

Mario and his fiancee Tegina were cruising down the aisles at Burlington Coat factory, shopping for coats for the upcoming winter. As usual, Mario had his cell phone up to his ear, conducting what he called business. Tegina and he had had several arguments about him and his incessant use of that damn phone. Tegina's point was she has a phone too, but when she is with him spending quality couples time together, she puts hers away. She thought that he should show her the same courtesy. She didn't mind if he got a call that was an emergency, she understood that, because if she got one that was an emergency then she would answer hers too. Anybody or anything else she would just return their calls later.

If Mario hadn't been so busy running his mouth on his phone, then maybe he would have noticed what she noticed. There were two men, probably undercover store security officers, standing in separate aisles, stalking him and watching his every move. Tegina could see it from her vantage point, they had separated and were in different sections of the store. She walked into the women's restroom and reached inside her purse, pulled out her phone, and dialed Mario's phone. He answered and said "Where did you go? Why are you calling me on the phone instead of coming back to me?"

Tegina said, "Shut up and just listen, bae. Keep talking to me on the phone while you are looking through the clothes."

"Girl, what are you talking about? Just come back over here. Where you at anyway? I hear an echo of your voice."

She said, "Mario, just trust me, do as I ask you. Continue to shop and look through the racks of clothing, but as you do so, every so often gaze up and around you and tell me if you notice the short man in the black shirt and the slender man in the gray shirt that have been following you around the store."

Mario did as Tegina told him to do, and in a matter of minutes had caught the both of them eyeing him, then trying to nonchalantly blend in as shoppers. Mario confirmed to Tegina that her suspicions were true. He told her that he wasn't worried about them though, they probably were just theft prevention officers who thought that he was just another black man trying to shop lift. He then told her to come out from wherever she was calling him from so that they could pay for their items and get out of there.

Twenty minutes later he and Tegina were standing in line at the register, getting ready to pay for their stuff. The cashier at register 4 rang up their total; it came up to $267.19. He pulled out a large wad of money and handed it to the cashier. The young girl cashier kept counting the money he had just placed in her hands, but gave him a strange look at what he said next. Mario stated loud enough for everyone in close proximity to hear, "You can tell your theft prevention guys that we ain't stealing," and then he pointed in the direction of the guys that were following him around the store earlier.

The two guys he pointed out were visibly embarrassed by being exposed by Mario. They then walked away in separate directions and disappeared into obscurity. The cashier finished counting Mario's money, placed it into the cash register,, counted out his change into the palm of his outstretched hand and then grinned, as if what Mario had said earlier was the joke of the day. Mario was wondering why she found it funny that he had just exposed her co-workers. So he asked her, "Why are you laughing? If I could spot y'all theft prevention officers, then I know a real shoplifter could see them from 100 miles away."

The young girl laughed again and said, "That's what's so funny. Those guys you just pointed out and embarrassed don't work here."

Mario and Tegina both laughed simultaneously and in unison said "Sure they don't.".They grabbed all of their purchases and headed out of the same door that one of the embarrassed theft prevention officers had disappeared through moments earlier. They went and loaded all of their purchases into Mario's luxury SUV, hopped in themselves, and then peeled off onto Colonial Drive, headed back to Windemere.

Immediately after they got out of sight, two embarrassed men sitting in the parking lot of Burlington Coat Factory in an inconspicuous government-issued van with dark-tinted windows, got out. They then walked back inside the Burlington Coat Factory, one of them wearing a black shirt and the other one a gray shirt. They walked past the help desk and headed right back to register 4, where the young girl cashier gave them a look of bewilderment. Although she had people in her line and someone at the register that she was ringing up, the short man wearing the black shirt pulled out his badge and announced that they were Federal Agents and they needed to get the purchase receipts from the guy who had just exposed them. The young girl, clearly amazed at all that was going on, did as she was instructed.

Shanell

Shanell had a busy weekend planned for herself. She was on her way to the K.T. concert being held at the Amway Arena in downtown Orlando. She and everyone else were very excited because at no extra charge at all, local Orlando rap star Mook Boy Fly Goon was added to the marquee after doing a short stint in prison. All of the local hip hop and R&B radio stations Star 94.5, Power 95.3, 104.5, XL 106.7 were flooding the airwaves every hour on the hour about this concert. Shanell was anxious to get out a little and enjoy herself, plus she wanted to show love and support for Maddy's friend K.T. and the rest of the artists from Orlando. She was also very anxious to be meeting up with sexy ass BA Boutthatlyfe. They planned their first meeting, or if you want to call it a date, at the concert. After the concert she was going to hit the road and drive the two and a half hour drive up to Tallahassee to go meet up with Maddy for FAMU's Homecoming game against South Carolina State.

Shanell pulled into the downtown parking garage, parked her car, got out, and texted BA Boutthatlyfe to let him know that she had arrived at their designated meeting place. Two minutes later he texted her back letting her know that he had already arrived and was near the front entrance to the concert waiting for her there. That brought a smile upon Shanell's face. She was happy that this younger man was on point and on time. She had heard many horror stories about dating younger men. She made her way down from the parking garage and made a beeline to where BA had told her he was waiting for her. When she got closer to the front door she scanned the crowd but couldn't spot him anywhere. So she pulled out her phone and texted him. "BA, I'm out front where you told me to come, but I don't see you anywhere, where are you and what are you wearing?"

After no response for three minutes, Janell began to worry about giving him credit for not playing games earlier. Then all of a sudden, a big burly muscular security guard came outside of the concert and yelled "Aye yo, is there a Shanell out here?"

At first Shanell was a little reluctant to raise her hand, but the security guard yelled the same thing again two more loud times and was scanning the crowd as if whoever Shanell was had better step up and show herself. Just then her phone rang and she looked at the screen and saw that it was BA Boutthatlyfe. She answered quickly and said, "BA, where are you?"

There was a bunch of noise in his background. Instead of answering her question he had one of his own. He asked, "Who is that I hear yelling your name?"

"I don't know him, it's some big club bouncer calling for some other girl with my name because we don't know each other."

BA quickly said "Yo Ma, put your hand up, cause I just paid him $20 dollars to come and get you out of that long ass line."

The bouncer spotted her with her hand raised and came through the huge crowd and got her and brought her into the concert. He walked her to the front of the line, took her ticket, handed it to the ticket woman in the booth, and then pointed Shanell to where BA was waiting on her. When she walked in Tonii Boii was performing "Pull Up," making the crowd at

Amway Arena go wild. She walked in, dancing her way over to where BA was, as Tonii Boii was screaming at someone to pull up on him. Sexy ass BA Boutthatlyfe was looking good even in the dark, wearing all white, creased pants, a Tru Religion hat with his dreads hanging nicely from up under it. When he spotted Shanell dance-walking his way, he smiled a sexy gold fronts smile that you could see very well in the dark. They bumped and grinded for Tonii Boii's performances, also when Mook Boy performed "Juvy," "Mohawk Shit," and "Windshield Wipers." All the way till K.T. stepped on the stage with his shirt off to perform his hit songs "Last Days," "Truth Be Told," and "Dead or Alive" they had one epic night of dancing, kissing and making out inside the concert. After the concert ended and before Shanell hit the road headed to Tallahassee, they made plans to get together when she came back into town. BA walked her to her car in the parking garage and gave her one of the wettest kisses in recorded history to see her off. Damn Shanell thought to herself as she drove off, "Damn! Is this what I've been missing?"

Sonic

Barry had tears flowing down both sides of his face. He knew that in a short period of time he would cease to exist. He had come to grips with this fact, had prayed and asked God to forgive him for his sinful lifestyle, and had asked his Son Jesus Christ to be his Lord and personal Savior. At this precise point in time he welcomed death, because he was in so much pain and agony. His life, his choices, and his family all flashed before his eyes. He was a 31-year-old man who was raised in the church, but never truly allowed the church or God into his heart. He never met his real father, who was rumored to be a military man that lived overseas, and his mother didn't have any boyfriends or men around him coming up.

Barry grew up on Texas Ave and Americana Blvd, and without a male father figure around he joined at the age of 11. By the age of 13 he was a full time drug dealer, because it wasn't beneficial for him to be gang banging and broke. He had been in and out of prison 3 times for sales and delivery of a controlled substance. Twice the substance was crack cocaine, and the other time it was MDMA (Molly). He had gotten out this last time three months ago, and although he had three years probation, he got fronted some drugs from an old neighborhood friend the day he got off the Greyhound bus from Madison Prison up near the Florida panhandle. That's how he had met this fool that had him bound and tied up at this very moment.

Much of his clientele were strippers from the clubs on OBT, trick hoes and prostitutes that wandered in from off OBT, and the neighborhood freak hoes. He served a lot of women, and he liked it that way cause when they didn't have money to buy his drugs, many of them were willing to trick with him for it. Shay, a stripper whom he had tricked with one time before, had brought this mad man with her about a month ago, when she came and bought some powder cocaine and some Mollys from him. He had a bad feeling about this dude the very first time she brought him with her to cop. This guy was too quiet and standoffish. He felt the same kind of vibes from this guy that he had with troublemakers he was in prison with. The one time that he had tricked with Shay, they had gotten high together and she gave him some of the best fire head he had ever had. He knew that she knew he wanted to get with her again, but ever since she started bringing this silent freak around, she was acting like they had never done anything before. That bad vibe that he would feel when this guy came around, now he knew that his senses were correct.

He had never wanted to come off Americana and come down here to the Budget Motel and bring this girl the drugs she called and ordered. First of all he knew that everything off OBT was hot and crawling with undercover police. He would usually meet them on Texas Ave or sometimes Rio Grande and sell them their drugs. But now he knew that that bitch Shay had set him up. He had told her over the phone that he didn't feel comfortable driving up OBT with drugs, especially coming to that hot ass hotel where she stayed with that strange quiet dude. Shay convinced him that all he had to do was drive the speed limit up OBT and use his signals properly and he would be just fine. To add a cherry on top she told him that Sonic was out of town for a week to go and spend time with and check on his family out of state. He still felt uncomfortable and was protesting until she said, "Come on, Barry man, I'm spending $50 dollars with you, my nigga".

He sighed his resignation and she hit him with, "I'll spend $50 dollars with you and sex you."

Barry replied, "What room number did you say you were in?"

Kei Kei

For two straight days after she went to Lake Mann Gardens look-ing for him, Super Dave spent time with her. They laid up under each other and had sex and spent quality time together. He even took her and Prince to the Magic Mall and bought their son a cou-ple of outfits. Kei Kei was feeling back on top of the world. Just 3 days ago she had risked breaking curfew and violating the terms of her probation for him, because she loved her baby daddy so much. After the way he had stroked her for two straight days no-body couldn't tell her lil young ass anything negative about him.

It was Saturday morning and Super Dave had left after he had gotten another phone call from his ace Teddy. After he got off the phone with Teddy, Kei Kei knew that he was about to get in the wind. But that was cool with her, the way that he had come and slung sausage for the last two days she was straight. While she was up under him though she didn't get on Facebook or any other so-cial media. They watched movies, had sex, ate order-out food and kept repeating this cycle for 48 straight hours. So guess what Kei Kei did in the absence of her man? She logged on to her Facebook account. While she and Super Dave was spending time together for those two days she took many pictures of them together. She started uploading them from her phone onto her Facebook page. With the click of a few buttons she had uploaded a picture collage of 16 pictures of herself, Super Dave, and their son Prince. In a matter of minutes the "likes," emoji's and comments started flooding in up under her picture collage.

One thing that we all have learned about Facebook and Instagram is we all have people on our friends list that are also friends with other people not on our friends list that we don't kick it with. People started tagging other people in the picture collage, and then the comments started pouring in like a broken dam. Emojis of wide eyes, LOL's. Pictures of Kermit the Frog drinking his tea and saying he's just minding his own business. People were posting memes saying "I'm just here for the comments," because the comments were beginning to be lit.

Kei Kei was confused why so many people were acting surprised and posting unsavory comments about her man Super Dave, a man whom she had been with for 3 years and had a son with him. Then she saw where her messy friend Arucha had tagged some girl named Otisha into her pictures, and then the negative comments kicked into second gear. Otisha wasn't mad at the pictures Kei Kei posted of Super Dave and herself, she knew that Super Dave had hoes and fans. It was funny to her because he was chasing behind her, not the other way around. But she was super petty and she knew that being the diva she was, hoes couldn't stand the fact that their men were coming for her, she wasn't coming for them.

Otisha posted some pictures of herself and Super Dave that they had taken on many of the occasions he came knocking on her door. She also downloaded a picture collage of 20 pictures of them. Captioned at the top of the picture collage, she stated "Your MCM is my side nigga." When Kei Kei saw these pictures that were downloaded for the world to see of her man, her baby daddy, her bae Super Dave in various states with this high yellow bitch she almost lost it. There were pictures of them in the bed together. There were pictures of him fast asleep in her bed captioned "Ooops I did it again, he's out for the count." There were pictures of them at the movies, of them at Fun 'n Wheels. And a couple of them on cruises and on casino boats. And even one of them in the front entrance of the apartment complex of this little high yellow hoe Otisha, and it was the same place she went in search of him at a couple days ago, Lake Mann Gardens.

Kei Kei's mind was all over the place. She thought "So this is the little hoe that he be missing with and ducked off with." Right then and there Kei Kei knew one thing for certain and two things for sure. One was both Super Dave and this yellow bitch Otisha had her fucked up. The other was both of them were going to have to straighten her when she saw them next.

Mario

Mario was hanging out in the black hub of Orlando, the Washington Shores Shopping Center. He was inside the Vietnamese store, picking up one of their famous delicious grilled chicken and shrimp salads. The Washington Shores Shopping Center is recognized in Orlando as a great place to go and get a bite to eat. You could also shop at a black-owned clothing store, get a haircut at On Every Occasion Barbershop and Beauty Salon from Chris Roc, BB, Rubena, Red, or Judy. Or you could get your teeth checked by the black dentist Mr. Willie B. Sherman, or go and sit up under the trees and play dominoes, poker, tonk, checkers, or chess. While Mario was standing in line waiting to pay for his salad he saw at least 10 people that he was friends with on various social media sites. Many of them came and went after they got their orders. He made it all the way up to the front of the line and paid for his salad and a bottled water and then headed for the door.

When he got to the door he grabbed the handle to push it and exit, but as he pushed someone was pulling to gain entrance. He quickly let go so that they could get in and in stepped Slimbaby Kia. He hadn't seen her since their threesome with Tina a week ago. They both looked into each other's face and paused, smiled, and just as Mario was about to say something to her, her eyes darted back over her right shoulder and she darted by him with a solidly built dude coming in right behind her. Mario caught on and stepped outside the store, but looked back to give a cursory glance as they stepped past him and into the store. When he glanced back, he glanced right into the mean mugging stare of Kia's fiancé, Efrem. Mario quickly put his phone up to his ear as if someone was on his line. If at that precise moment someone had decided to call him he would be exposed and Efrem probably would have jumped on him right there right now. But being the character that he was he played the little charade to the tee, he said into his phone "Yeah, bae, I'm at the Shopping Center getting us a salad." Then he turned and walked towards his drop-top Chevy Chevelle.

Efrem stood in the doorway of the Vietnamese store with the door wide open, looking at Mario as he walked away to over where his dunk was parked. Mario soaked this attention up, he knew that this dude was watching him, plus some other folks who had seen this exchange were tuned in to what was about to happen next. He made it to his car, threw the phone that had probably just saved him from getting his ass beat into the front passenger side of his car. He opened his driver's door, sat in the front seat, and cranked his car up, just before he put it in reverse to back it out and leave. He pulled his big gold chain from beneath his collared shirt, and cranked up the bass from the amazing sound system that he had installed in his donk. He put his $1300 dollar Cazal shades on, pulled away from the curb, looked over at the door where Efrem was still standing watching him, mean mugging him, laughed, and drove out of the Washington Shores Shopping Center jamming Mook Boy's West Orlando anthem "Mohawk Shit." He loved the envy and hating of males just as much as the jocking and thirstiness of the females. He was in a zone listening to his childhood friend Mook Boy go off. He zoomed past Ivey Lane as he hit the accelerator heading down Raleigh, passing Carver Shores with Mook Boy yelling about the boys that wore the mohawks.

Sonic

Somehow Barry managed to make it to the Budget Motel without any police or undercover police stopping him. Shay had given him an extra incentive to come to her room, and he drove up Rio Grande, turned up 18th Street, and crossed OBT via 18th Street and arrived safely. He didn't like coming down here. Every time he got arrested and was in 33rd Street jail he heard all of the horror stories from other inmates about how hot OBT was. But the thought of serving Shay $50 dollars worth of drugs and getting free head thrown in as a bonus was too much for him to pass up. He pulled into the parking lot of the old motel and got out and walked up to the room number she had given him over the phone. He knocked on the door, and when she opened it he saw another warning sign that he totally ignored, because he was too busy entertaining a visual of her on her knees giving him some more of that awesome head that she had once put on him. He stepped inside the motel room and noticed that there was clear plastic all over the floor, and covering most everything but the bed. At first sight Barry started to protest and ask questions, so he said "Ay yo, what's up with all of this plas?" but Shay caught wind of his uneasiness and made the move to quell his fears.

She was wearing only a thong and skimpy top that didn't do a good job of holding down her tits, or her nipples for that matter. She walked on top of the annoying plastic and went and sat on the bed and patted it, motioning for Barry to come and sit down next to her. She said, "Nigga, come on over here and let's take care of what you came here for. Take your pants off and come here, Barry."

He said "Now that's what I'm talking about," totally forgetting about the plastic all over the place.

He took his pants off and walked over near her on the bed. Shay said, "Nigga, where my drugs at? I want to take a hit before I have sex."

Barry picked his pants up off the floor and pulled out a baggie with cocaine in it. Shay noticed that he had baggies with cocaine, weed, mollys, heroin, and a large wad of cash in those pants that were on the floor. He handed Shay a quarter bag of raw uncut cocaine. She opened it up and made herself a straight white line on the nightstand right next to the bed. She took a hit and then held her head back as the narcotic began to enter her blood stream and invade her senses. She motioned for Barry to step closer to her. He did and she leaned over and took his penis into her mouth and went to work on him like she was Superhead's sidekick. In a matter of minutes she had him moaning and squirming right there standing beside the bed on all of that plastic. Shay was a true headhunter and she was reminding Barry of just why he had taken the risk of coming here in the first place. She was working him and still getting high. Every now and then she would stop sucking him, then lean over on the nightstand and make another one of those white lines she had made disappear up her nose. The cocaine really had her wired. She was really into the oral pleasure she was giving Barry; she was making animalistic noises as it seemed like she was enjoying it just as much as he was. The animalistic noises she was making was turning Barry on even more. She was slobbing, gargling, and gasping all while looking up at him like she enjoyed every thrust and stroke into her mouth. She stopped sucking for a quick second and said, "Damn, Barry, this some good ass shit you got. This shit makes me horny!"

Barry was enjoying it too. Just then he thought that he heard a noise behind them. But Shay's mouthwork was keeping him focused on what was in front of him, kneeling in front of him. Slob, spittle, and animalistic sounds made by Shay spurred Barry to keep going and disregard the unmistakable subtle sounds that were coming from behind them. Then he heard it again and turned the upper torso of his body and saw a shadow move in the unlit part of the room. Undeterred, still sucking and still making animal noises, Shay kept doing what she did best. Then he heard it again louder this time. Someone was in the room with them. Barry turned around and looked straight into the face of the quiet, crazy guy, standing in the dark, leaning against the counter, watching as Shay continued to give him head. He was standing there in the dark smiling, holding a gun in one hand and a pick axe in the other. This made Barry freeze up, but Shay kept sucking. Barry thought to himself how in the Hell did this fool get in here. He looked down at Shay who was still on her knees giving him sloppy, noisy head with her crazy boyfriend standing 10 feet away with two weapons of death in his hands. Barry knew then that this bitch had set him up.

Kei Kei

Tanya angrily crawled out of the bed from with her on-again, off-again boyfriend Nate. She didn't want to move or be bothered today because she was booed up with her man, but she kept hearing her grandson Prince crying for some reason. She opened her bedroom door with a hard swing and stormed towards the living room where she heard Prince's cries coming from; she wanted to see just why he was keeping up all of this ruckus. His Mama was supposed to be watching him and spending time with him. Tanya came down the hallway and into the living room wearing her night gown, fluffy house slippers, and an attitude. When her grandson Prince spotted her he immediately ran to her and started tattling on his Mama Kei Kei. He said in his baby dialect that was broken, "Mama Kei Kei hit me," and pointed his little finger at his Mama who was on Facebook posting statuses about no good dog ass niggas.

Kei Kei looked up from her phone and said, "That's right. I popped his little bad self. He was out here getting into everything, won't listen, and was sassing me."

Tanya looked over at her teenaged daughter and shook her head as Kei Kei had her head down, scrolling Facebook on her phone. Tanya said to Kei Kei, "Well, maybe he wants your attention, some of that same attention you're giving to Facebook, Kei Kei."

Kei Kei said, "He's just so bad, Ma, and won't do nothing I tell him. So I popped his little behind."

Tanya said, "You were the same way when you were that age too, girl, running around getting into everything. But the difference between you and him is that you knew who your mama was when you were almost 3. He doesn't. You need to spend more time with him and not have your face buried to your phone on that Facebook and Instagram mess, Kei Kei. It's a shame that your son thinks that you are his sister and not his mother, and that needs to change, Kei Kei."

Prince was now crying and begging for Tanya to pick him up. Tanya bent down and picked her grandson up, then looked back over at her daughter who still had her head down typing a post on Facebook. She was responding to some other girl's response to her post that she had made about dog ass niggas ain't shit earlier post. Tanya walked across the room with Prince in her arms, she crossed over to where her daughter was sitting with her face glued to her phone and her Facebook page. She stood behind her with Prince still in her arms whining and read what Kei Kei was posting and some of the comments that the other girls were posting back.

Tanya said, "Girl, this is why you can't pay your son any attention, and in here popping him, because you and all these little girls on here man bashing your men, sounding like a Mary J. Blige song. I'm your Mama and I'm going to always keep it real with you. You're running around here losing sleep and time that you will never get back over that no good ass Haitian, who ain't much of a father so I don't know why you'd think he would be a good man. Don't you know you're young, fine, and beautiful and can have anyone you want? Girl, the best way to get over one man is to get under another one. Here get your son, I always have him."

Tanya bent down and handed a now-screaming Prince to his Mama. She said, "I'm going back to my room and get back up under my man."

As she turned to walk away her grandson was hollering and yelling for his Mama, who was holding him, but he didn't know any better. He thought his sister was holding him, and he continued to cry and holler for his grandma, who he thought was his mama. Tanya walked back down the hall to her room, opened the door, and as she was closing it behind her she heard Kei Kei telling Prince, "Hush, boy, with your spoiled self. Uuugghhh."

Mario

The old man was coming through Orlando today, and Mario was supposed to be meeting with him at the truck yard. He had called Mario three days ago and told him that when he traveled through Houston to pick up his load, he would be picking up Mario's order as well. Mario let him know that he would be ready when he made it to Orlando. At 10:30 the old man called him and let him know that he was coming through Ocala and would be in Orlando at the truck yard around 12:30 or 1 o'clock. So Mario went to eat breakfast at a place he ate at all the time (and he had even gone live there on several occasions), Soul Food Fantasy, where the breakfast, lunch, and dinner specials were always hot and always appetizing. He knew the owner Tina; he had tried to run game on several of her attractive friends Margie, Kiesha Black, and Angel. But none of them fell for his shenanigans, because all of them had husbands that had prestige and money as well.

He went in and placed his order, kicked it with Tina and her staff for a few, then when his food was ready he shot home and took Tegina the breakfast that she had him order for her. They ate together and talked about the upcoming field trip that had to be paid for in order for their daughter to be able to go. Then as time got closer and closer to when Mario was supposed to go and meet the old man at the truck yard, he told Tegina that he would see her and their daughter later on tonight, he had some business to attend to.

Parked inside the gated community with their car backed into a neighbor's yard, of course with the neighbor's permission, as well as the armed guards at the front gate of the gated community, two inconspicuous DEA agents were watching the comings and goings at Mario's residence. He kissed Tegina bye, walked out the door and got into his luxury $40,000 dollar car, logged onto his Facebook page on his phone and backed out of his driveway. He drove right past the two DEA agents backed into his neighbor's yard. There is a high likelihood that he could have spotted them had he not been scrolling down his timeline on Facebook, even though these same two DEA agents switched cars daily to follow him.

Mario was paying too much attention to his "posts" "likes," and "follows" to see that he himself was being followed in real life. By the grace of God Mario made it to the truck yard while paying more attention to Facebook than he did to the road. He hopped out of his Benz, eyes still glued to his phone. He pulled out his keys and opened the door to the trucking business that had two trucks in the yard that hardly ever moved. The two DEA agents pulled into a busy shopping strip directly across the street from the truck yard, parked, and were watching his every move.

Three days earlier, their boss, along with a Federal Prosecutor for the Middle District of Florida, walked into a Federal court and convinced a Federal Magistrate to allow them to wiretap Mario's cellphones, business phones, and home phones because he was a part of a criminal complaint on a criminal enterprise that they were investigating. The Magistrate signed off on it after viewing the compelling evidence that the DEA had stacked up against Mario.

The DEA agents were listening in when Mario called the old man's phone, to let him know that he had already arrived at the truck yard. The old man then let Mario know that he was coming through Clermont and Winter Garden on the Florida Turnpike now and would be there in less than 30 minutes.

Mario hung up and went back to his Facebook page. He saw where there was some more new thirsty hoes all in his inbox. Some of these chicks were saying all of the things that they would do to him sexually. One said she would suck him dry, another said she would suck him to sleep, then another one was talking about eating his ass like groceries. He always found these thirsty hoes funny, but they fueled his ego like he had a full tank. Just then he had an idea. He reached into the black satchel and pulled out a $10 thousand dollar stack of money and put it to his ear. He pulled out his phone and took a picture like this and downloaded it to his Facebook and Instagram pages. He sat back and watched all the "likes," comments, and emojis piling in while he waited on the old man to deliver his dope.

Shanell

Florida A&M's homecoming game was everything Shanell had hoped it would be. She had so much fun spending time with her daughter Maddy, whom she had missed very, very badly while she was away in college. They were all over Tallahassee club hopping, mall hopping, just like old times. Tallahassee was electric. FAMU had beaten Howard on a last-minute touchdown pass, and the whole city was in party mode. There were several planned club events and after parties set for tonight. Shanell and Maddy couldn't make up their minds on which one to attend. Shanell and Maddy, mother and daughter, and partners in crime were reunited together, for a weekend. Later on that night they still hadn't made up their minds as to which after party club event to attend, so they started driving by all of them to see which one was the livest. Tallahassee is a town that has hills all over the place, and they were all over town, up and down hill they went, turning corners and enjoying being back together again.

Shanell's phone rang, and when she looked down at the screen she was happy to see that it was BA Boutthatlyfe calling. She had been having so much fun at Homecoming weekend she had forgotten to stop and give him a call, as she had told him she would. She answered her phone "Hey, Bae," and Maddy looked at her and scrunched up her face as if her Mom had broken one of the Ten Commandments Moses came down from Mount Sinai with.

Shanell looked back at Maddy, stuck her tongue out at her as if she were saying na na na nana boo boo, and kept talking to her bae. Shanell told BA Boutthatlyfe that she was having such a great time with her daughter Maddy that she had forgotten to call him. They talked for a few more minutes before Shanell promised to call him later on. Before she hung up she also promised to come and see him when she got back in town on Monday.

After she hung up the phone with BA, Maddy was all over her like a TSA security guard at the airport. She said "Are you serious Ma, bae already? Didn't you just meet this dude?" questioning Shanell as if she were the child and Maddy was the mother.

Shanell replied, "Maddy it's just a term of endearment, it's not even that serious."

Maddy shot back, "Not in this new era, Ma. You just can't call any and everyone Bae. Do you realize that Bae is short for Before Anyone Else? You shouldn't be calling newbies that you just met that. Slow down with this dude, Ma, I'm worried about you and how fast you are moving with this new dude."

Shanell didn't think that she was moving too fast, but she was not about to go back and forth with her daughter and ruin the great time they were having together. Besides she knew Maddy had her best interests at heart. She thought to herself, it's not like she had went and had sex with the man, but she also knew that part of Maddy's protest was just loyalty to her father, Domonique. Shanell knew without a shadow of a doubt that her only child loved her. But her daughter was 218 miles away from her now, living in another town, attending college and making a new life for herself. She loved Maddy, but Maddy wasn't there with her anymore, especially on those lonely nights when her bed was its coldest. Coupled with that was the fact that this sexy younger man was interested in her and showing her all of this attention. She hadn't had affection and attention in a long, long time. She told her daughter Maddy what she wanted to hear, she told her that she would slow down and take it nice and slow with this dude BA Boutthatlyfe. But in reality her foot was nowhere near the brakes, it was on the gas, and when she got back home to Orlando she was goning to apply more pressure to that gas pedal.

Sonic

Barry had heard the stories about people being frozen with fear, but he didn't understand that dilemma when told by others until now. He was stuck, couldn't move, frozen in fear. He was standing there looking into the eyes of a deranged lunatic that was holding two weapons, smiling sinisterly as his girlfriend's head bobbed up and down in front of Barry. At that very moment Barry couldn't stop Sonic from killing him, or Shay from giving him head. He was helpless. Without moving much he tried to break the ice. "Wh, wh, what's up bruh, how'd you get in here?"

Sonic said sharply, "Nigga, don't worry about all that, go ahead and get your last nut before you leave this world."

At the thought of dying today Barry immediately got weak in the knees and began to cry and beg for his life. Shay kept sucking. He fell to the floor in fear in the prostrate position, messing up Shay's sucking groove. She protested, saying "Hey!" and looked at him as if he was being rude for not allowing her to finish.

Barry, not fazed about messing up Shay's groove, kept his eyes on Sonic and those two widow-making weapons that he wielded. "Please, bruh, please don't kill me, man." He then started to testify to Sonic against Shay, "Man, this wasn't my idea, it was that bitch's idea, bruh. I asked her where you was and were y'all still together. She told me that you had left town, man."

Sonic looked down at Barry cowering and begging for his life and laughed at what he had just said as if it were a classic Kings of Comedy joke. He looked at Shay who was bent over the nightstand, making another white line disappear up her nose. He looked back down at dry snitching Barry and said, "That bitch right there told you all that homie?" pointing his gun at Shay.

Barry, who now looked as if he had found a newfound hope, perked up and said, "Yeah man, that's what I am trying to tell you, that bitch did this messy shit."

Sonic looked back over at Shay who was apparently higher than an astronaut on a ladder and said, "Good job, baby. Now go get me this nigga's pants and let's see what he donating to us today."

Shay laughed, wiped her nose and mouth, and then got up and went and retrieved Barry's pants for Sonic. Sonic rifled through the pockets of Barry's pants as Barry sat in fear on the floor where he had damn near collapsed earlier. Still holding the gun just in case Barry tried something, a big smile came across Sonic's face. He counted $1,741 dollars cash, $2,500 dollars worth of cocaine, $2,000 dollars worth of MDMA (Molly pills), and $750 dollars worth of high-grade marijuana.

Sonic told Shay, "You see, baby, that's why I told you to call this duck ass nigga. I knew that he would come through for us. I see the way he looks at you and acts whenever he serves us. He always pulls out all of his money whenever he serves us, trying to flex, and fucked around and put a target on his own back. I told you he was going to bring us a huge donation when he came here, didn't I?"

Shay said, "Yeah, baby, you were right, because you did say that." She walked over to the small hotel mini fridge and pulled out a bottled water. She walked past a begging and pleading crying

Barry and went to his stash that Sonic laid on the table next to him. She pulled two Red Monkeys from the Molly stash and popped one in her mouth, took a swallow of water, then turned and placed one in Sonic's mouth, then gave him a swallow of water. The ecstasy enveloped his senses like some does a burning building; his insides were on fire, but his senses were dulled by the drug. He motioned for Shay to move out of his way.

Barry began to beg, cry, and plead again but Sonic was unfazed. He was a cold-hearted killer when sober; today he was a sub zero murderer on an amphetamine. He said, "Nigga, pick a spot in here where you wanna die at, anywhere but the bed. This plastic is for you. It's gonna catch your body, your blood, and any other DNA that you may leave behind."

Before Barry could pick a final resting place, Sonic shot him between the eyes, chopped his body up into small pieces with the pick axe to make it easier to get it out of the room and dispose of it. He and Shay rolled it up in some of the plastic and gave the room a thorough cleaning. Still high off of the Red Monkeys, Shay put her pretty mouth to good use on Sonic; after all that killing, blood, and drugs, they were both high and horny.

Kei Kei

Kei Kei was a bit nervous as she sat in her probation officer Mrs. Washington's office, listening as Mrs. Washington read off several violation-worthy offenses to her and her Mama Tanya. Her GPA had fallen, and she had several tardies to school and classes. Mrs. Washington had gone by CEP and talked to several of her teachers who had told her that Kei Kei could do much better, if she just applied herself. They told her that Kei Kei had honor roll and even valedictorian skills, if only she would put as much effort into her schooling as she did with other things. She showed flashes of brilliance on one hand, and then disturbing periods of ineptitude, laziness, and attitude. Mrs Washington did not want to violate Kei Kei and have her locked up. She realized that this young lady was wasting her potential. So instead of making her another inmate with a jail number, she gave her a longer leash. She said, "Keiyanna, if I were to give you a urinalysis test right now, do you think you could pass it?"

Kei Kei shook her head no, she knew if she were to be tested the test would show high levels of THC. Mrs. Washington then turned to Tanya and asked her how things were going at home between her and Kei Kei, and Kei Kei and Prince. Tanya lied and said everything was good at the house. She didn't want Prince to lose his Mama and what little connection they had. She was helping Kei Kei raise him, and he thought she was his Mama and Kei Kei was his sister. Things between Tanya and her on-again, off-again boyfriend Nate was on and popping at the moment and she was enjoying her quality time with him.

Mrs. Washington wrote something down on Kei Kei's monthly probation report, typed in the computer on her desk for several minutes, and then abruptly got up and walked out of her office without saying a word to Kei Kei or Tanya. This made both Kei Kei and Tanya a bit nervous and jittery. A few minutes later they heard voices coming back down the same hallway that Mrs. Washington had just disappeared down. Tanya stood up and peeked out of Mrs. Washington's office and down the hallway. She exhaled deeply as Mrs. Washington, another probation officer, and two uniformed Orlando Police officers came walking back down the hallway in their direction. Tanya sat back down and waited for them to come and take her daughter away and out of her and her grandson's lives. Tears began to form in her eye sockets. Kei Kei noticed this and asked, "What's wrong with you, Ma?"

Tanya told her what she had just witnessed coming down the hallway. Kei Kei grabbed her Mama's hands to calm her down, and told her, "Ma, don't worry about me, everything is gonna be alright," as a tear formed in the corners of her eyes as well. She stood and gave her Mama a tight hug as she heard the voices getting closer and closer to arrive and come and place her under arrest.

Mrs. Washington grabbed the door handle, twisted it, and came back into her office. Kei Kei stood as she came back into the office, ready to face the consequences. Mrs. Washington looked at her and said, "All right, Keiyanna, I will see you next month, and you better get clean because I have to give you a urinalysis, so you better not smoke any weed, girl."

108

Kei Kei smiled that pretty smile of hers, exhaled, and said "Yes, ma'am."

As Kei Kei and Tanya walked out of Mrs. Washington's office, the two officers that Tanya had seen coming down the hall earlier were now coming out of the probation officer's door two doors down from Mrs. Washington's office with a young girl that Kei Kei used to go to Evans with in handcuffs. Her name was Simone, and just like Kei Kei, she had a young child too. She had violated the terms of her probation after failing a urinalysis test. Some people catch breaks and some people don't. Kei Kei and Tanya watched as the Orlando police placed the handcuffed teen mother Simone in the backseat of the squad car and pulled off with her. They looked at each other gave big sighs cf relief and jumped in Tanya's car and headed home.

Mario

Mario had a good hearty laugh as he went through his Facebook friends list, looking at the many photos that some of these women post on their own walls and press send for other people to view. He had many of these same women on secretly recorded video; he thought that this was funny. He was a pompous undercover hater who acted macho to hide his insecurities, and he had several insecurities. He was the son of a father who was old enough to be his grandfather when he was born. Mario's father was almost 60 years old when he was born. He had brothers and sisters that were in their 30's and 40's when he entered this world. His mother at first was the fine neighborhood teen that used his dad as a sugar daddy, but after falling on hard times and getting kicked out of her mother's house, she ended up having to move in with her sugar daddy and start giving him the sugar for free. Seven months later, his 19-year-old mother was pregnant by his 59-year-old father. A year later his mother was strung out on crack, and running from her 60 year old abusive lover.

Mario's father took care of him for the first five years of his life, but after with deteriorating health, he allowed young Mario to go and live with his mother's older sister, who had kids older than Mario, but was better equipped to raise and spend time with him. His mother's side of the family was really huge. He started meeting all of the many cousins that he had. His father's side of the family was huge as well, but he was his father's old age love child so they sort of kept him a secret from that side of the family. When he did meet someone from his father's side it was either brothers and sisters old enough to be his dad or mom, or nieces and nephews that were older than him too. He lived with his mother's sister until he turned 17 and met his son's mother while out in his neighborhood selling drugs. They immediately moved in together and after two months she found out that she was pregnant with his child.

Mario was a fast learner and a great hustler; his come up was swift and lucrative. He went from nothing to something fast and that's when the flossing flashy lifestyle was born. Quanda, Mario's first love and babymama, noticed his change and arrogance and confronted him about it several times without success. He wasn't trying to hear it and his response to everything and everyone that didn't agree with him was, "You're all just haters that's hating on me because I ain't broke no more."

Fourteen months later Quanda paid for Mario's flashy flossing lifestyle with her life. A woman disguised as a Fed Ex delivery driver knocked on their door one day, and when Quanda answered the door, the woman pretended to have some packages that needed to be signed for. Quanda, reaching for a pen to sign for the packages, was surprised when the woman came up with a gun pointed at her. She then forced Quanda back into the house, where their sleeping son was. After the woman gained entry she called someone on the phone and in 5 minutes there was a knock at the back door where the woman opened it up and let two goon looking men in. The men came in and started ransacking the house turning things over and breaking valuables. This enraged Quanda and she began to protest and berate the men as the woman stood there in her living room with the gun aimed at her. Quanda began to get into a verbal jousting with one of the male robbers, and after they found a couple thousand dollars, they got anxious and told Quanda that she had better tell them where the rest of her flashy boyfriend's money was. She laughed at them and mocked them and he shot her at point blank range in the face.

Mario had taken a break from the limelight after moving away for a little while, but now with the invention of social media sites like Facebook and Instagram, he was back to his flashy flossing lifestyle with an even bigger audience. Attention was the new currency and he couldn't get enough of it. He had a sense of pride that was actually arrogance in disguise. He was obsessed with the need to be important in the eyes of others. That was the spearheading factor on why he always posted all of those floss videos, even though it had cost someone he loved their life. Because he spent a large portion of each day trying to figure out ways to impress or shock his followers and friends. Mario was a self-centered chauvinist and attention whore, and he was going to remain relevant by any means. That's why he made and kept those hidden videos of all of those women that were in relationships. Those videos empowered him, making him look at all of those unsuspecting men as if they were chumps for falling in love with these hoes that he had on a string. He logged onto his Facebook page and posted a video about how he was a godly man that turned his life around, owned businesses, and was also a community activist. He smiled that sly smile that he smiled when he knew that he would get a bunch of "likes," "pokes," and inboxes for his video post. He knew gullible, "looking for love and a man" females always fell for the religious God-fearing, God-loving man routine.

Shanell

Shanell sat inside Tip Top nail salon near Orlando's famous Magic Mall, getting a manicure and pedicure. She was on her off day from her job and was using it to get cute for a night out with her new boo BA Boutthatlyfe. They were going to go and see Ride Along 2 starring Ice Cube and Kevin Heart. Afterwards they were going to head to Bahama Breeze to eat and sit around the Tiki bar and order drinks. Anything after that, they were just going to go with the flow. After Shanell finished getting her mani and pedicures, she walked through the huge parking lot and went to the Magic Mall to see her childhood friend who owned a tattoo shop inside the Magic Mall. He was also a local rap celebrity, but as he got older he smartly invested his money into owning his own business. She walked into his shop, and he and his wife Melissa were tag teaming some artwork onto a young man's neck. At first they were so immersed into their work that they didn't notice that she had walked in. Melissa noticed Shanell first, and then she said, "Baby, look what the cat just dragged in."

He looked up and smiled at his childhood classmate and friend. He hadn't seen her since Maddy was a small child, but his smile indicated that he was happy to see her. They had one of his new hit singles playing in the tattoo shop. It was called "I'm a Star," and his rap name was Preacher. As kids he and Shanell both loved Hip Hop; they would both be involved in dance contests as kids at Funtastic Skating Center.

115

Melissa stopped helping Preacher with the young man's neck tat and walked over and gave Shanell a hug. She said, "Girl, what are you doing coming by the shop?"

Shanell told her that she wanted to stop by and have her and her husband help find a nice tattoo for her right shoulder. She had invited BA to come up and chill with her while she got pampered, but he quickly declined saying that he never stepped foot inside of nail salons. He went on to say that nail salons were worse than barber shops when it came to gossip and rumors. Shanell thought about Maddy and her stern warning to her about slowing down and taking her time with this dude BA, who seemed to have Shanell's nose wide open. She sighed as she thought about slowly backing away from this handsome, fine younger man just to allow one of these younger thirstier females to snatch him up.

The competition for a good looking fine man was fierce in Orlando. With the invention of Facebook and other social media sites, you had to do all types of things to keep a man or get a man, Shanell thought. Even though she was new to a lot of these sites, she had watched way too many downloaded videos of females willing to do threesomes to keep a man, strippers were taking a lot of women's men, and many females were proud side chicks that bragged about getting wifey treatment. Shanell just wanted her very own man. If she were to wait on Domonique she would be an old maid by the time he got out. She was going to let loose a little tonight and let her hair and her inhibitions down a bit. Ff something happened between her and BA tonight, then so be it. She wasn't going to throw herself on him like some of those girls that she had seen on some of those videos on Facebook and Instagram, but she wasn't going to deny nature from taking its course by being bougie and stuck up like she didn't need, want, or desire to be touched by this sexy man either. She caught goose bumps and felt all warm inside just thinking about this fine tatted man working his body all over hers.

Sonic

Rent was caught up and paid up at the Budget Motel on Orange Blossom Trail for a few months. Sonic had just came back to the room from the front office. He placed his receipt on the table and sat down. Shay passed him the boonk blunt filled with a mixture of marijuana and cocaine. He took it out of her hand and pulled hard on the lethal mixture blunt. They had enough drugs to last them a couple of weeks; they had enough to sell half of the drugs and still get high for two weeks.

But Sonic was a drug fiend robber, and a homicidal maniac, not a drug dealer. Sitting here getting high, after paying his motel bill up for a month in advance was spoils of war for Sonic. It didn't bother his conscience, his sleep, or his day-to-day activities that he had murdered many people in like fashion, by brutally murdering and dismembering them. In his outlandish wicked mind he was ridding the world of human vermin.

Barry wasn't the only victim he had chopped up and disposed of the body parts in different sections of a city; he had done it a time or two when he was still living in Detroit. He had learned from watching his favorite television show *Dexter* that it was hard for law enforcement to build a case without a body. He was in his element on OBT; he loved the chaotic atmosphere that surrounded the area. There was so much going on that the OPD couldn't just focus on a single problem. Sonic fit in well here. It reminded him so much of his hometown Detroit. Both cities were similar in size, and both cities had a high crime rate where murders went unsolved and into the cold case files with high frequency. People went missing all of the time, some on purpose because of the illegal activities that they were involved in. As a matter of fact in Sonic's mind being in Orlando was much better than being in his hometown Detroit, because in Detroit he was a known threat. But here in Orlando he was just another strange face passing through as a tourist or visitor. He was a faceless killer in Orlando that no one knew personally. In Detroit he was lil Jasonic the stickup kid that was known for squeezing the trigger. He still owned the element of surprise in Orlando.

Sonic took another hit of the boonk joint that Shay had rolled and fired up. At this point in his life, neither NA nor many of those drug rehabs that other addicts paid a small fortune to attend would do him any good. Getting high helped him keep the demons in his head at bay; they weren't so bad when he was high, drunk or both. He pulled out his laptop and logged on to Facebook to check some of his traps and saw that flossing dude Mario had downloaded a video claiming that he was a God-fearing man. Sonic wanted this guy so bad that he could taste him; he was begging someone to rob him. And Sonic was going to answer his call. He knew what he was going to do to Mario would make headlines at *The Orlando Sentinel*. Just as other serial killers before him, Sonic enjoyed killing people in cold blood, and this guy Mario's murder would be talked about down here in Central Florida for a long time. Sonic would admire his handiwork through the news outlets and the local newspapers, just like John Wayne Gacy and Ted Bundy used to do. Yeah it's good that you are a God-fearing man, he thought about Mario to himself. Fear is a great motivator, and soon I will see it in your eyes, flosser.

Kei Kei

Otisha was in Pine Hills on North Lane at her Mama Trina's house. She and Latima had come over to drop off three garbage bags filled with designer clothing that they had boosted. Her phone was blowing up—she was supposed to be meeting this girl named Jessica who kept calling her repeatedly up at Haji's Quick Stop store to bring the girl Jessica a Tru Religion outfit.

Sitting in the parking lot at Haji's Quick Stop waiting for her to pull up were Kei Kei, Jessica, and Ashley. They had devised a plan to put in an order with Otisha, the high yellow bitch that Super Dave was messing around with, and when she got there Kei Kei was going to confront her and jump on her about her baby daddy and the pictures she had put on Facebook. They would also take her merchandise. It wasn't like the hoe could call the police; she had boosted and stolen it her damn self. Kei Kei was tired of these hoes disrespecting her. There was no excuse for this new little yellow bitch, even though she and Kei Kei weren't friends everybody in town knew that Super Dave was her man. Plus the pictures that this hoe had downloaded and captioned proved that she knew he had a lady and a child.

Jessica's phone rang and after she looked at the screen and saw that it was Otisha calling, she put one of her fingers up to her lips and made shhhhh sound to Kei Kei and Ashley. She answered and Otisha came on the line and asked her, "Where you at? I done made it to my Momma's house down on the other end of North Lane."

Jessica told her that she was parked in the parking lot in front of Haji's store. Otisha told her to give her a few minutes and she would pull up on her. Jessica hung up the phone and looked in the backseat at Kei Kei and said, "You ready, bitch?"

Kei Kei winked her eye at her friend and continued to put her weave in a ponytail bun. "Girl, I am about to drag this yellow hoe when she pull her ass up in here."

Three minutes later, a big blue Ford Explorer pulled in with a sexy middle-aged high yellow woman with tattoos all over her body and gold teeth in her mouth driving. She pulled up and Kei Kei, Jessica, and Ashley looked at each other and said "Nall, that's not Otisha."

They knew that she drove a cream-colored Lexus because it was all over her Facebook page. Then all of a sudden Trina got out, then Otisha got out of the front passenger seat, Latima got out, and then three more of Otisha's cousins jumped out. This changed everything, Kei Kei could fight, but being outnumbered 6 to 3 made her cancel that dragging that she had in store for Otisha. Jessica knew two of the cousins and didn't want to fight or video any fights at this precise moment. Ashley just sat there looking like Lucky the Puppy, she was on her phone talking to some boy that most likely was someone's man, being the hoe that she was known to be.

Seeing that things could take a turn for the worse, Jessica jumped out of her car and spoke to the two cousins that she knew before she asked, "Otisha, what's up? Tisha, you got my outfit?"

Jessica knew not to let Otisha come up to her car because if she saw Kei Kei then things could get heated. She loved to videotape other people's misfortune, not her own. Back inside Jessica's car Ashley was still talking to someone else's man, while Kei Kei was quieter than a church mouse, ducking down lower in the back-seat hoping not to be spotted and dragged by the yellow hoe and her kinfolks, the way she had planned to do her a few minutes ago. Kei Kei was still going to get this little yellow hoe, but just not today. This bitch Otisha had a huge family and it would be a little harder to catch her by herself than what she had planned. "Run, run, run away; live to fight another day," Kei Kei thought to herself as she peeked at Jessica and all of those hoes Otisha had brought with her. She wished Jessica would come on so they could get the hell away from here, and she wished Ashley would shut the hell up with all of that begging like a Keith Sweat song. She thought about Super Dave and all of this shit that he had her going through and another Keith Sweat song popped into her mind, "I knew you were cheating on me, baby."

Mario

Mario's Facebook inbox was just as busy and full of traffic as Orlando International Airport and International Drive combined. Ever since he posted a video of himself promoting and brokering a deal to bring Louisiana Rapper Lil Boosie to Orlando, his phones, his Facebook, and Instagram accounts were jumping like a kangaroo on a trampoline. As a matter of fact the two hottest topics on local social media were Lil Boosie coming to Orlando in a concert, and how Aaron Gordon got robbed at the 2016 NBA All Star Game Slam Dunk contest.

Mario was getting the attention and acclaim that he loved, wanted, and seemed to need so much, because the buzz around town was that he was the one bringing the hot famous Rapper Lil Boosie to Orlando. He even went on the "Go Live" app to show himself putting up fliers all over Central Florida. He was in Pine Hills, on Silver Star, in Rosemont, on Hiawassee, on Mercy Drive, on Old Winter Garden Road, up at Big B store on Ivey Lane, in Carver Shores, at the Washington Shores Shopping Center, in Merchinson Terrace, in Lake Mann, in Boca Club, Orange Center, Beirut, Apopka, Altamonte, Winter Garden, Sanford. Just all over the map, being both the money-getting hustler and the attention whore that he loved being. While most promoters preferred to work from behind the scenes he loved the shine of the limelight. He was more P.Diddy than Suge Knight.

He craved attention like the Reality show T.V. persona he saw himself as.

In three separate locations, two DEA agents, two cousins, and a serial killer were all watching Mario's posted videos simultaneously. All five of these men had plans to meet up with Mario soon and take him down a couple of notches, with his flossing ass. What Mario was failing to realize about social media was not everyone viewing your downloads, quotes, and posts liked what they were reading or seeing. Jealousy and Envy were first cousins that bought the worst out of many individuals. These five individuals who were plotting Mario's downfall were filled with the first cousins, Jealousy and Envy. Even the two DEA agents had grown tired of watching him flex, flaunt, and floss in real life and on the Internet. At first it was just a job to them, but to see the type of money he flaunted, the types of women that he snuck around with and the expensive wardrobe that he wore, these two DEA agents became full-fledged haters with badges that were making a case against this showoff. Mario had a lot of followers on Facebook and Instagram, but he was about to find out that everybody that was following you or friended you wasn't following you or friending you because they cared about you. Two people watching his video were out to indict him and throw him in prison, two were out to catch him and hurt him in revenge for creeping and sleeping with their fiancees, and one was out to kidnap, rob, and murder him so that it would make front-page headlines. It would also line his pockets for a very long time. In fact, he felt like Mario's donation would make Barry's look like a 10% tip that you gave your waiter.

Shanell

Shanell wanted for her and BA Boutthatlyfe to ride together just like the movie that they were scheduled to go and see, Ride Along 2. But BA had protested and insisted that they meet up at the movies, and then when they left the movies tail each other to Bahama Breeze. BA smooth talked his way into getting his way from Shanell, and she finally relented and backed off from them carpooling to the movies. She was just happy with the fact that they were going out together to have a good time and enjoy each other's company. This type of activity was what had been missing in Shanell's life. Yeah, she had fun with Maddy and her friends when they used to go and hang out, but that was in the past now ever since Maddy had enrolled in college.

She had not been taken out on a date by a man ever since Maddy was a small child, back before Domoninique was indicted. They laughed so much at the movie theatre that they were holding their sides. Kevin Hart was a fool and a modern-day Eddie Murphy. He was funny and getting on Ice Cube's nerves all at the same time. They both predicted that those two were such a good pairing that it was no doubt that it will certainly be a Ride Along 3. They were really enjoying each other's company, the dialogue between them was lively and fluid, and once the movie ended they decided that going to have those drinks together at Bahama Breeze was a great idea. They walked outside still laughing and discussing Ride Along 2 and the huge star power that Kevin Hart had amassed in the last couple of years. They also discussed the impact the Ice Cube had made on Hip Hop and now was making as an actor in Hollywood. Wanting to extend this date they decided to head to International Drive where Bahama Breeze was ducked off in the tourist district. A few minutes later they were up on I-4 with BA following closely behind Shanell as she exited I-4 on at the Kirkman off ramp and navigated through traffic towards Bahama Breeze. They arrived at Bahama Breeze and before long the Long Island Ice teas, the Ciroc with cranberry juice, and the Sex on the Beaches were being downed and refilled at a rapid pace. Both of their blood alcohol levels was officially above the legal limit; they were inebriated. They started kissing and touching each other like high school kids who weren't chaperoned properly. They both agreed to take this show back to Shanell's place.

The only problem was that both of them were drunk and not in the best shape for driving. They both knew that the Orange County Sheriff's Office and Orlando Police Department were both known for spotting and arresting drunk drivers out on the roads of Orlando. But fear factor, inebriation, lack of proper motor skills, OPD nor OCSO weren't going to stop these two from attempting to be together. They both made it safely to Shanell's house and staggered their way inside. Shanell was drunk but she knew exactly what she was doing at this point and time. She was about to have sex with the second man ever in her 39 years of living.

Sonic

Sonic had made several people beg for their lives during his kid-nappings, robberies, and eventual murders. Making them beg and plead for their very lives was euphoric and empowering to him. For the short period of time that he allowed them to beg and cry out to him, he felt a sort of godlike complex. He had become a serial killer: seeking, stalking, and carefully hunting and searching for his next victims. There were two other things that he loved to indulge in that were high up on his priorities list as well: hardcore drug usage and illicit sex. He was currently engaged in both.

He and Shay were in his room at the Budget Motel hav-ing a threesome with Jasmine, this little, short, thick-thighed stripper that Shay danced with at Flashdancers. They were all doing an assortment of drugs and drinking. These two women were bonafide, no-holds-barred super freaks, but the deadly mix of drugs and alcohol had made them even more freakier, if that were possible. When Sonic climaxed a couple of times and had nothing left to give, after they had drained him, Shay and Jasmine kept going at it without him. They went at each other like an old married lesbian couple. This was why Sonic preferred these types of women. They weren't stuck up or wor-ried and complaining about their hair, nails, or makeup. He knew that drug-addicted women such as these two that he was watching perform cunnilingus on each other, would get high and perform whatever sexual debauchery he asked of them without much complaint. He also knew that if he got them strung out and dependent on him for drugs, then they would build a emotional and dependent attachment to him. He could start getting them to assist him in setting up and performing his robberies and murder. That's what he and Shay were doing now. They were not only exploiting Jasmine for her body today, they were about to tempt her to become their co-conspirator in setting up Mario for his downfall. Sonic had figured out that a guy with an ego as huge as this guy Mario's who posted all of his business on social media, was doing it for the attention and affections of females. Sonic laughed at Mario's flossing social media lifestyle and surmised that he didn't see how this guy wasn't in Facebook jail, he was setting himself up for actual reality jail, and if law enforcement didn't come soon enough, his flossing flashy ways would have him deceased and on an "In Loving Memory" T-shirt.

An hour after all three of them had started, Shay and Jasmine were still going at it. It seemed as if these bitches had big energizer batteries installed in their backs. The girl-on-girl action between these women was a thing of beauty. This mixture of drugs and alcohol made their movements seem synchronized; they gave just as well as they got. The bed was wet, as if someone had taken a shower and laid in it wet and dried off. Watching them was turning Sonic back on. As Shay ate Jasmine out, the noises and moans that they both made woke up something inside Sonic that Viagra and Cialis had tapped into and charged men a fee for. Sonic got up and snorted another line of coke that Barry had donated a week ago. He walked over and slapped Shay on the ass as she was bent over eating Jasmine out. Jasmine was moaning fiercely as she lay spread eagle on her back, enjoying every inch of tongue that came out of Shay's mouth. Murder was his profession, he had never held down a job, filed for taxes, or cashed a check. He robbed drug dealers and made the majority of those he had robbed pay with their lives. He knew it would all end for him one day, but today he was going to get high some more, and have unadulterated sex with these two off-the-chain strippers. He dropped his boxers to the floor and went and laid down in the damp bed, where two women started double teaming him all over again.

Kei Kei

For all of the 5000 friends Kei Kei had, the 10,000 followers she had, she was sitting on her Facebook page doing something that she never did. She was holding a conversation with a male who had inboxed her. She had entertained a couple of boys at Meadowbrook and Evans when she and Super Dave had fallen out a couple of times, but nothing serious ever came of either instance because she was stuck on her Haitian baby daddy. But Kei Kei was growing tired of the constant disrespect and drama that he was taking her through. Kei Kei was a good-looking, fine well-shaped female herself. Super Dave pulled the stunts that he pulled because she was young, naïve, and in love. He knew that if Kei Kei were an older, more mature woman, then she would have taken their son and given him his walking papers. Kei Kei felt as if Super Dave had been bullying her over the course of their whole relationship, and she was about to do something about it. Not only was she holding an inbox conversation with this young man, she had sent him her cell phone number in his inbox. And now they were on the phone talking every day, sometimes late into the night. She was no longer calling and chasing behind her disrespectful Haitian baby daddy.

Pretty soon, just like in most cases, the streets started talking and word got back to Super Dave that his baby mama was talking to another man. At first he acted like it didn't bother him, but after about two weeks of Kei Kei not calling him, and him continuing to hear that the other man had Kei Kei catching feelings for him, Super Dave started popping up and calling a lot. He started threatening Kei Kei with, "You better not have no nigga's around my son" and if she would post something on her Facebook or Instagram pages about #TeamSingle he would make a slick or derogatory comment right there on her page.

Kei Kei was enjoying giving Super Dave a big dose of his own medicine that he had been making her swallow all of these years. She reached into her bag of tricks and pulled out an even bigger spoon to make him take some more medicine. She placed the other guy as her MCM when Monday came rolling back around. Nobody else in the history of her Facebook account had ever been her MCM besides Super Dave, and even when she was mad at him, no one else had ever held that honor until now. The crazy thing about this whole ordeal was Kei Kei sort of liked this other guy, but the truth of the matter is, she was using him as a pawn in this chess game that she was playing on Super Dave. Kei Kei had grown tired of crying herself to sleep and then waking up and having to wash the dried up tears from her face. It truly hurt her to hurt her baby daddy in such a deceitful manner, but this way was one of the only methods she had ever used over the years to make him give her the respect that she asked him for. Not only was he popping up at her house unannounced but so was Teddy and their other two homeboys, Hollywood and Brandon. They would come and pick up Prince and take him shopping themselves.

You know who else took note of all of these changes? Tanya. She told Kei Kei that she should have been stopped playing the fool for Super Dave. She said, "Girl, you are too beautiful and fine to be around here crying over milk that keeps spilling over on purpose. I ain't bragging but I know you got some good coochie, cause the apple don't fall to far from the tree."

Tanya then put her hands on her hips and went back in the room with Nate. Kei Kei's phone began to vibrate. She looked down at the screen and it said "Bae." She wanted to answer badly and talk to her bae (Before anyone else), but the way this psychological game of "pretend that I now have someone else" was set up, she couldn't show her hand. She kept her poker face on and let him go to the voicemail. He left her a voicemail message. She smirked out a smile. Before she gained the upper hand, he never left voicemail messages. Then a moment later the text messages, inbox messages, "pokes," and DM messages from him started pouring in. Yeah she had Super Dave up against the ropes, and damn did it feel good. Better him this time than me, she thought as she looked at the comments and emojis that started coming in after her MCM announcement.

Mario

Mario had just gotten an inbox message from someone, but what was strange about the whole thing was that it was from a dude. He always got inbox messages, but they usually came from the fingers of thirsty women. He was about to delete it when he recognized the dude in his inbox by his profile picture. It was the dude Superproducer Jay, the same dude that he had friend requested almost a month earlier. He wondered what he was talking about in his inbox and decided not to delete it, but read it instead. It said "Yo, what's up Bro? I see you're doing big things here in the City Beautiful. You actually beat me to the punch. I was thinking about bringing some big name artists to concert here in Orlando. Especially with the tragedy that happened here at Pulse nightclub. I know that we can get a headline event to come and turn the city up to full blast. I was thinking maybe trying to get the old Cash Money back together and bring them here with Turk, BG, Juvenile and Manny Fresh. If you're interested in making it happen hit me back in my inbox and we can schedule a meeting."

Mario liked what he had just read from the guy Superproducer Jay. He was down with all that he had said in his message to him. Truth of the matter was he didn't need Superproducer Jay, he had well enough money to make the Cash Money Records Reunion happen himself. But he was going to use this guy because he figured he was legit. He would use any legit person that he could attach himself to, to make it seem as if he were a legitimate businessman too. That was the only reason why he had friend requested and inboxed this dude Superproducer Jay; he wasn't a man fan. He was an opportunist. Mario inboxed Superproducer Jay back and told him that hell yeah he was interested in them pairing up and making the Cash Money Reunion a reality. But he would have to get back to him on setting up a meeting until after his Lil Boosie concert.

Superproducer Jay told Mario that he wished him well with his concert,,and to give him a holla afterwards. They both agreed and logged off. Mario was cool with it because he had the intention of using this man's good name to bring in some major money opportunities. All of his fake businesses were surrounded around him using the legitimate people he surrounded himself with. Lil Boosie was coming to town because of his money, but through his fiancee Tegina's name. If Mario had tried to use his fake businesses as a front for promotions he would have been exposed and indicted in less than a year. This was cool with Superproducer Jay because he was actually serial killer Sonic from Detroit Michigan, who robbed drug dealers. Mario had everyone else fooled, but he didn't have Sonic fooled. Sonic knew he had to be a drug dealer pretending to be a businessman, because he had stalked drug dealers all of his life and this guy fit all of the protocols of one. In this new Internet era, legit businessmen did not floss and take pictures with money because they were usually working too hard to make it. They didn't need to be showing social media all their money so that they could come and rob them. Drug dealers in this new era were always flashing money, jewelry, clothes, and status, and with their bravado they also flashed guns and weaponry and dared someone to try and come and take it from them. Sonic knew that when he set up that page as Superproducer Jay, that one day Mario flossing ass was going to come a calling. Money attracted money in this new era.

The more you had, or acted like you had, the bigger your friends and followers list. He thought that Mario was going to make an even bigger donation than Barry had made. What Barry had donated was going to be like a server's 10% tip compared to what he was expecting to get from flossing ass Mario. Watching this inbox conversation exchange with much anticipation were two jealous, envious DEA agents who had been assigned to follow Mario, tap his phones, and monitor his social media accounts. They were watching, listening, and recording, and now wondering who Superproducer Jay was and what he and Mario had to do with each other. Right now they didn't know, but they were watching, listening and recording to see.

Shanell

BA Boutthatlyfe had given Shanell the best oral sex that she ever had in her life, but Shanell still felt halfway satisfied. She wanted the sausage too. It had been a long time since she felt Domonique inside of her. She wanted BA to get up inside her, but he was in her bathroom throwing up and unable to hold down the alcohol that they had consumed earlier at Bahama Breeze. Shanell was helping him in every way that she could; she was genuinely concerned for him, but she also wanted him to get better and give her the sausage too. One minute he's bent over between her legs licking and eating her to ecstasy like an ice cream cone, then the next after she tells him that she wants to feel him inside her, he's bent over the toilet as if it was the god that he prays to.

Shanell surmised that she wasn't a drinker and she wasn't do-ing all of this throwing up, so maybe just maybe BA was less a drinker than she was. Now she was happy that they hadn't car-pooled. If they had, then that would mean that she would have had to drive his drunk ass home. What started out as a beautiful evening together was ending in a somewhat disappointing fash-ion. Shanell didn't want this man to be sick, she wanted him to be well and inside her. Yeah, she was being a bit selfish, but she figured anyone with a sexual deprived deficit such as hers would understand. But someone who was getting them some on a regular rotation would have something slick to say about it.

Shanell walked into the bathroom and asked BA, "Bae, are you gonna be alright." Leaving it as an open-ended question just in case he could make a miraculous recovery and return to the bedroom and give her what she wanted and needed so badly.

BA, still slobbering and holding on to his porcelain god said, "I don't know, baby, everything is spinning."

Shanell said, in a last-ditch effort to get what she needed and wanted so badly, "I have some Pepto-Bismol in the medicine cabinet, maybe that can help you."

BA said, "Naw, baby, I feel like I'm seasick on a ship. Shanell, have you ever heard of a sickness called vertigo?"

Shanell said "No, what the hell is that? Am I safe? Is it contagious?" Then she thought about all of the warnings that Maddy had given her.

BA sensed her concerns and quickly cut in, "No, no, no, it's nothing like that. It's not a sexually transmitted disease, it's a sickness that starts in the inner ear". He explained the whole vertigo process to her in detail.

Afterwards Shanell wasn't all that interested in having him inside her, she was too worried about all of the slow-down warnings Maddy had given her. She wasn't going to stop seeing BA Boutthatlyfe, but she would take her daughter Maddy's advice and pump on her brakes a little. She helped BA get up and get his bearings together, walked him to his car, and promised to get with him a little later. BA was apologetic and promised her that he would make it up to her soon. Then he jumped into his car and sped off.

Shanell was confused a bit about all that had just happened, but she was happy that BA was well enough to get up from off the bathroom floor and hugging her toilet, and make it to his car.

She walked back inside her house and made her way over to her nightstand next to her bed.

BA had ate her box as if it were a Popeye's $5 fill-up and he sure knew what he was doing. But he left her desiring to be filled up, so she reached for the only man that had entered her besides Domonique: her big black dildo that she had named Sampson. She clicked Sampson on and he sounded and vibrated weakly. She told Sampson "Now I know you ain't about to leave me hanging like BA just did."

She looked around to see if she had any batteries to give Sampson a jolt of electric Viagra. There were no batteries anywhere in the house. She hadn't stopped by any stores for batteries in months. Frustrated, she was just going to go to bed with the oral pleasures that BA had given her. Then by the stroke of a quick pick lottery selection, she turned the T.V. on and remembered that the remote control contained batteries as well. Now if the batteries from the remote were the same size as the ones Sampson needed then she would be back in business. Three minutes later Sampson was purring long and strong and Shanell was moaning while holding her own legs over her head, as if Sampson were the man of her dreams.

Sonic

The advantage that Sonic had on Mario and all of his Facebook friends and followers was he wasn't who they thought that they were following. The profile picture attached to his Superproducer Jay account was not him, it was a photo of someone none of his followers knew. Slow Money, the actual man in his profile picture, was up north in a Federal Penitentiary doing a long prison stretch. Mario and most of these new age flossers on the other hand had their life pictures as their profile picture on their accounts.

The difference between Sonic and these new age hustlers was they wanted to be known and seen, he wanted to remain anonymous. They were interested in making some noise out there in the streets; he moved in silence. They preferred background singers, entourages, or teams; he was a solo act. When Mario went most places in Orlando people recognized him from Facebook or Instagram; when Sonic went most places, no one knew who he was.

Mario and his main man Jon Jon were hanging out at this new hot spot hangout called the Lowkey Lounge, where they served breakfast, lunch, and dinner. They had pool tables, video games, card tables, dart boards, T.V's on all the walls and a big light-up dance floor. A lot of people from Orlando were flooding to this new place because it was a nice little relaxing place on Orange Center Boulevard owned by a friend of Mario's from Carver Shores named Lovis. Jon Jon was racking the balls again while Mario loudly talked trash to him. They were playing $100-a-game 8 ball. Mario loved attention, so after every ball he knocked in, he damn near did an Odell Beckham Jr touchdown celebration. His fat friend Jon Jon from east Orlando was just the opposite of him, he was laid back and quiet and didn't even have a Facebook or Social Media account. He racked the balls, stayed quiet when he won and paid Mario when he lost.

Lokey's was packed and this was right up Mario's alley. Inside the crowd of spectators watching Mario carry on like a peacock were several people he recognized on his friends list. Also watching was a person who was on his friends list that he didn't recognize or even know. That was the good thing about Sonic being lowkey, inside of Lowkey's lounge, watching and stalking Mario. One thing performers had to understand was that they could always at any given time get up on stage and perform, but they didn't always know who was in the crowd watching their performance. What the hell was Sonic even doing in a place like the Lowkey Lounge? He was completely out of his element. He didn't hang out or mingle, especially in places where his face could clearly be seen by others. Although he was there with Shay and Jasmine stalking Mario, he still didn't like being out in a public place where people could approach you at any given moment. In certain areas of the Lowkey Lounge it was heavily lighted, over near the pool tables where Mario was loudly playing and performing for the crowd, it was lit up considerably.

The only reason why Sonic and the strippers had stepped foot in this place was because Mario had gone on "Go Live" an hour earlier and had announced that he was going to go and hang out at his childhood friend Lovis's new spot the Lowkey Lounge on Orange Center Blvd. Sonic and the strippers were there to give some attention to the man who craved and loved it so much. Two haters with government badges had watched Mario's "Go Live" feed as well and decided to go and see what all of the fuss at Lowkey's was about. They would soon find out that Lowkey's Lounge was a semi-sophisticated spot that had security at the entrance to the front door that patted you down every time you walked in or left and came back. Lowkey's had an older crowd of patrons.

Mario sank the 8 ball again and the inner Cam Newton in him surfaced. He started dabbing and bringing extra attention to Jon Jon and his table. "Yeah nigga rack em up."

Jon Jon was tired of this man, his mouth and his mannerisms. He reached into his pocket for his phone and purposely speed dialed his wife Savonnia. Savonnia picked up on what her husband was trying to do, because she knew her husband did not like to be in the spotlight. She just listened as Jon Jon pretended to carry on a conversation with her. He said, "Alright, baby, I'm coming, but I did tell you that I was gonna step out for an hour or two."

She then heard Mario's fat mouth say in the background where there was a bunch of noise, "Man, fatboy, you probably called your wife to keep me from diggin' further down in them pockets."

Jon Jon said, "Naw, man, we promised our daughters Dewey and Jayla that we would take them to Cheddars for dinner tonight. I will catch up with you next week after your concert is done man." Jon Jon then headed for the exit and the parking lot.

His wife Savonnia had warned him many times about this social media showoff Mario. She had Facebook and Instagram accounts too and always saw things that he either posted or was tagged in. In her opinion a man doing the things her husband and Mario were doing had no business posting the type of flamboyant things that came across her newsfeed. She knew that this guy Mario was seeking attention and asking for trouble all in the same sentence. She just didn't want her husband to be around him when the people who threw surprise parties came calling, the ones in the ski masks, or the ones in the alphabet jackets.

Walking a few feet behind Jon Jon headed out of Lowkey's as well was a tall lanky DEA agent. He hid in the shadows and filmed it as Jon Jon got inside his white Dodge Charger, exited the parking lot of Lowkey's, and turned right heading east onto Orange Center Blvd. He snapped a photo of the tag on the white Charger that Jon Jon was driving. They would check the national database, and see if they could find out who this fat smooth dude who was hanging around this known drug dealer Mario was. Some people love pictures and attention; some people loved to fly below the radar and not be seen, heard or known. But if they go and meet up with someone who loves attention as much as Mario does, then they unknowingly get pictures taken of themselves, and surveillance put on them like Jon Jon just did.